MORE PRAISE FOR

Light Box

'Poignant, observant, profound: K J Orr's stories – like waves against a breakwater – bristle with tremendous, barely concealed power.'

D. W. WILSON

'A globe-trotting wonder: atmospheric and haunting, delicate and fierce. Orr writes with radical precision and beauty, and this collection shines a masterful light on the quiet, often unseen moments that have the power to remake a life.'

LAURA VAN DEN BERG

'I'm pretty sure Orr only begins a story if and when she can sense in the idea of it the makings of a crisis – which then, with forensic precision, sentence by sentence, questioningly, she uncovers. This is invention in the old meaning of the word: the discovery of what is there to be found. And that finding is persuasive and disturbing in equal measure, like truth itself.'

DAVID CONSTANTINE

'With microscopic delicacy, Orr unravels our human longing for certainty and order in these exquisite, devastating stories, revealing the chaos that is both the tragedy and the joy of being alive.'

TANIA HERSHMAN

'These stories are by a brilliant writer. She creates her worlds in perfect prose, faultlessly, for the reader to walk through – creates paths that, once walked, will never be forgotten. I have no doubt that these will become modern classics.'

VANESSA GEBBIE

'These stories move from Buenos Aires to the American East Coast and across to Tokyo and the heartland of Russia: they are beautifully formed and contain powerful, vital moments of transformation that light up in pitch-perfect prose.'

MAHESH RAO

'A wonderful and assured read, brimming with coolly controlled writing that is mysterious but never purposeless. Each story contains enigmatic, piercingly clear images and startling gestures that illuminate its characters in all their passions and furtiveness.'

COLIN BARRETT

'Orr is an absolutely natural short story writer who knows that life's profundities often unfold without witnesses, beyond the action of centre-stage, in the private language of instinct, fumbled need and fleeting connection. Her stories read with a compellingly cool clarity and restraint. They are also thrillingly precise. *Light Box* is, above all, a luminous collection. It reveals, with beautiful acuity, what it is to be human, tender and fallible.'

ALISON MACLEOD

'Orr is fascinated by the power of strangers to forever alter the trajectory of our lives. In these stories, chance encounters threaten to destabilise relationships, inspire treacherous voyages, and reveal the fissures on which our identities are constructed. The language is scintillating, the insights piercing. A stunning debut.'

ADAM MAREK

'Orr's is a distinctive new voice. These stories are so elegant and considered, yet charged at the same time with a fierce energy.'

TESSA HADLEY

K J ORR

LIGHT
BOX

stories

DAUNT BOOKS

First published in Great Britain in 2016 by
Daunt Books
83 Marylebone High Street
London W1U 4QW

2

Copyright © K J Orr 2016

A CIP catalogue record for this title is available from the British Library.

ISBN 978-1-907970-74-0

Text designed and typeset by Tetragon, London

Printed and bound by T J International Ltd, Padstow, Cornwall

www.dauntbookspublishing.co.uk

For M.

CONTENTS

LIGHT BOX

'Talk about a view,' the woman said. 'Will you look at that view?'

He acknowledged her comment with a nod, but did not speak.

'Will you look at those clouds?' she said.

He was looking. He didn't have much choice. The train was crowded, and he was standing shoulder to shoulder with this woman and a line of others, their backs pressed flat against the wall of a sleeper compartment, leaving just enough space for people to squeeze past along the corridor. He was facing the windows, as they all were, by default, bags tucked behind legs. The woman was to his right. Conversation might have seemed more natural to her than silence, but he didn't want to talk. He wanted to be curled up in a seat by himself in a corner somewhere, asleep.

The rail tracks ran so close to the river he felt they were skimming the surface of the water and that any moment they would all be sucked into a chaos of water and air. The river reflected a mass of high clouds – great puffs, cotton balls, blinding white, a spumous procession.

'When I see weather like this,' the woman said – she spoke slowly, giving each word weight – 'when I see clouds like this, you know, I think of my husband, my George.'

She shifted beside him. Cramped as they were it was a small adjustment of weight on feet. He sensed her looking at him – and so she was, her head tilted awkwardly against the wall. There were tears in her eyes, but she was smiling and had a guileless expression on her face.

'He passed three years ago, almost to the day, and it was just like this. So very beautiful. I couldn't help feeling it was a sign.'

The way he was standing he could feel his toes pressed hard against the ends of his shoes. He moved his feet a fraction. He fixed his gaze on them.

She kept talking.

'And when my grandson asks where his Papa has gone, and what he should do when he wants to talk to him, my son says—,' and here she paused for a moment, swallowed, 'my son says, "Anytime you want to talk to him you just look up at the clouds. Look up at the clouds."'

The young woman to his left was deep in her book. Intermittently, depending on the play of light, he saw her reflected in the window. She had a smile on her face, which could have been the book, or the situation; either way she didn't seem inclined to help him out.

He could turn to her, a plea in his eyes.

He could lower himself down the wall, slowly; in his bag, propped behind his legs, there were things he could fetch. He could take a step forward, towards the window, and turn around to pick the bag up.

But it was beyond him. He let his head fall back against the compartment wall.

'You look tired,' he heard the older woman say. 'Are you tired?' He could feel the pressure of her arm where it rested against his. 'But you have lovely skin. You must have been told that. You must have been told that many times.'

He had closed his eyes and now he opened them a fraction, but he didn't respond. His stomach was furious with acid. He wished he had food.

'Do you have a regime?' she said. 'For your skin?'

He shifted his head without lifting it from the compartment wall. She wasn't looking at him, he found, she was staring out of the window at the view, but when she sensed the movement she turned once more and beamed straight up at him, her eyes still damp.

'No,' she said. 'Silly question. You're too young for a regime.'

He thought to make his way to a washroom. He thought perhaps he could shake her off. But an attendant, now, was making her way down the corridor, taking reservations for the restaurant car. She was substantial. Her progress was slow. People were adjusting bodies and feet as best they could.

'I got five, a quarter after, five-thirty, a quarter of, six,' the attendant said, at volume, nasal, as she arrived in front of them. She had a buzz cut and pale, peeping eyes. She was so wide she seemed to be addressing both of them at once.

'I'd like to eat early,' the woman beside him said. She turned to him. 'Do you mind eating early?'

'I'm not eating,' he said.

'Come now. Young man, I would like to buy you dinner. It would be a pleasure. What time shall we say?'

'I'm putting you down for five, okay? For two,' the attendant said. 'What name? Gotta move on. Got a lot of folks.'

'Joanie,' the woman said. 'And five is just perfect.'

Maybe she was getting off the train, he thought. She was so keen to eat early. It would be surprising if a woman of her age were going any great distance without a seat.

The train was working its way up the river. They passed a string of small stations, platforms only a few metres long, hovering close to the water. They passed the old prison, its walls worked over with barbed wire and weeds. Nearer to Manhattan he had seen a flotilla of white sails on the far side of the Hudson, the New Jersey side, but nothing since. The towns they passed seemed emptied out – parking lots with no cars, deserted streets dividing rows of neat, quiet houses.

Joanie had fallen silent. For the moment she was watching the world coursing past. Now and then, an intake of air as she braced herself against the motion of the train, the jolting back and forth.

A change in the land beyond the river, to wooded hills.

When the train slowed and they pulled into a station, the carriage juddering and becoming still, he remained a long moment, palms flat behind him, pressed against the wall.

'You have a half hour, folks. Half an hour.'

People were manoeuvring past, filing along, bags hugged to chests. And then the corridor was clear, and they were gone. Joanie too.

On the platform he gratefully breathed the fresh air.

He made his way up a flight of steps towards the facilities, following the throng from the train. There was a water fountain outside the washroom and he drank from that, splashed his face. Heading back to the platform he was following his hand, skimming his palm along the smooth rail that ran beside the steps: Joanie.

'It sure is a long way up!' she said. She was hauling herself one step at a time with the help of the rail. He took her in: the roomy, low-cost, middle-American clothing. The hair, which must be grey or even white, dyed caramel and coaxed into a wave.

'Do you want a hand?' he asked. He was unable to stop himself. The words just came out.

'Oh no! You are a very lovely young man, but this is *good* for me, this is *necessary*. Look around at our nation, won't you?' She pulled herself up another step so she was level with him. 'Fatties!' she said, bugging her eyes. '*Look around.*'

He didn't look around, and neither did she. He waited until she started moving again, and then continued down to the platform, leaving her on a slow upward trajectory.

Passengers were standing alongside the train, stretching their limbs, sipping coffee or sugary drinks. There wasn't much to see. On one side the view was blocked by the carriages, and on the other there were railings, another empty lot, a thin row of trees.

A flurry in the leaves of the trees and it started to rain. It didn't matter. They were all under the cover of a walkway. He watched the rain fall, soft and thick and wet, adding a slick sheen to the expanse of asphalt opposite.

'Would you see that!' Joanie was at his elbow, face angled to the sky. 'Oh I knew it!' She was jubilant. She was actually clapping her hands.

He could see what she saw: just visible in the rheumy air, faint above the gunmetal parking bays, a rainbow. Joanie was gripping the railings with both hands. 'Isn't that something?' she said.

It wasn't much of a rainbow. He had seen better.

'When we buried my George,' she said, clapping one hand to her chest and spreading her fingers wide, 'when we buried my George, a rainbow just appeared in the sky.' With her free hand she reached out and touched his arm. 'A perfect rainbow. *Perfect*. Right. Over. His. Grave. I had been waiting for a sign and there it was.' She was looking into his eyes as she spoke and when she had finished speaking she kept on looking. Tears were coming. She was trying to smile but the smile turned into a grimace and then she let out a series of sobs. Suddenly she pulled herself in towards him and pressed her face into his chest. People were watching. He brought up his hands and saw them stop, poised, just above her head.

When it was time to board the train once more, the carriage guard – who had also been watching – came forward and, assuming they were together, offered them seats in the compartment he used.

Joanie nodded her head, attempting a smile and wiping her eyes with the edge of one hand, still clinging to him with the other: her weight on his forearm, his bag slipping from his shoulder, a trail of warmth on his skin from the pull of the strap as it slid down the length of his arm.

Caught up as he was – a seat, perhaps, even so, he thought.

The guard showed them the way, leading them along the cramped corridor where they had been standing, to the sleeper where he had set himself up – the fold-down tabletop laid over with neat rows of Amtrak ticket stubs, and brochures, and timetables.

'You are a nice man,' Joanie said.

She was sniffing, but seemed to be over the worst. As if to confirm it, she flashed her teeth in an approximation of a smile, took a sharp breath, sighed, and settled into a seat.

'Well,' she said. 'Would you look at this.'

He had found himself in Times Square that morning, had stood bathed in colour, had closed his eyes.

When he opened them, there it was: a vast animated hoarding with a moving image of a woman. She was looking down – at the street it seemed – and holding one finger to her lips. She was deciding.

He hadn't slept and it had taken him a moment to understand what was going on. Those people looking up at her were being filmed, so they appeared on the screen somehow, in miniature, like minions at her feet.

The giant woman held her finger and thumb like a pincer, suspended. She would move her hand so these jaws would rove and stop, rove and stop. They would be poised all of a sudden above a person's head like a threat. A smile on her lips.

It was random, pre-recorded, but it looked like intent. A cluster of tourists close by were tracking her hand, moving about so that it might be them standing beneath. The camera zoomed in to pick out faces. Each time: a cheer from the street.

And there he was. He was suspicious-looking, shifty. This look he now had.

The giant woman above him, scattered laughter, he had tried to cover his face with his hands.

The sleeping compartment was smaller than he would have guessed. The seat backs and curtains were blue, and everything else was grey. Everywhere there were levers and tilts and multi-level sections of surfaces serving different purposes. There were buttons to be pressed in yellow and blue and red. There were arrows up and arrows down. There were signs of warning – *Caution!* – and a row of stubby red lights, alerts of various kinds related to the sink, mirror and toilet. A bed suspended from the ceiling blocked the upper half of the window. The second bed, he thought, must be made up somehow from the seats, with the table pushed back. The two seats faced each other. Joanie was in the one facing forwards. He was watching the world slip away behind the train.

The guard's handiwork was laid out on the table between them like a hybrid of Monopoly and Patience, careful lines of overlapping counterfoils with route stops stamped out in caps: BUFFALO, NY; ERIE, PA; SOUTH BEND, IN.

Joanie opened a route guide. It was large enough to obscure her face. 'Henry Hudson,' he heard her murmuring behind it, 'The Wonder Years. General William Jenkins Worth.'

Putting the guide down, she inspected their surroundings. She pointed out a narrow post-box slit that sat between them underneath the window. 'That,' she said, 'is where the table folds into.' She nodded to herself. She looked past his head to the compartment wall. 'See all those lights?' she said. 'They have a light for everything.' She squinted. 'They have a reading light. They have a main light. And they have a mirror light.' She turned her attention to her own seat, glancing down and about, animated, like a snuffling creature of some sort on a hunt. She had been resting her arm on what appeared to be a step to the top bunk, but with a little encouragement it flipped up and she found herself looking at a metal funnel. 'Oh my, it's the john!' She let the lid drop and sat back.

He wished she would wash her hands. From where he was sitting he could see that a sink was hidden just above her head – flagged by hand towels and wrapped bars of soap – but she hadn't seen it.

He tried to focus on the magazine that he found in his hands, that he must have picked up somewhere. The feel of it: the gloss tacky against his palms. He saw her looking. He rolled it into itself, made a tube of it. It was a women's magazine.

As the train lurched, the door to their compartment slid open and shut, open and shut. Across the corridor, in the compartment opposite, a pair of legs was visible from the knees down – pale chinos, buffed brogues.

'He did not!' a woman's voice exclaimed, loudly.

'I swear to God,' came the dry response.

'He did *not*!' the woman exclaimed again.

Back and forth the door went, back and forth. Across the way the pair of legs uncrossed and re-crossed – fingers drummed on one knee.

The door opened and shut. He started counting it: gave it numbers.

One, two; he counted.

One, two.

One, two.

'Okay,' Joanie said, making a face, swiping an invisible something from the air with one hand. 'Would you mind? Would you mind latching that?'

There was a hook you could slip over a nub of metal to secure the door. He was able to lean from his seat and flick it into place. Now the legs were obscured. The voices were faint. It was just the two of them.

It had started a couple of months in. He hadn't noticed at first. He had been aware instead of changes in his hands. His fingers developed blistered patches – tiny, swollen, liquid puffs. He noticed these before the counting. He bothered them. He broke the surface of the skin to let the liquid out. And then the counting. Once he had noticed the counting he watched himself doing it with an awareness that seemed to offer nothing in the way of helping him stop.

One, two.

One, two.

Like breathing.

Joanie's head fell back against the seat, and in a short time she was snoring softly.

Through the window he watched the rail tracks multiply and diminish, the telephone wires running overhead. He looked beyond the tracks to the water, and beyond the water to the land opposite, the dense woodland hills.

Joanie's breathing had changed. It was heavy and slow. With the door shut the sound was amplified. It seemed to him that the whole compartment was breathing with her, that he was locked in the humid cavern of her chest.

Looking up, he was surprised to see she was awake and studying him.

'Why have you locked the door?' she asked. Her voice was querulous. Her eyes were small and scared. She was pushing her hands downwards on her legs in a rhythmic way, like a cat working the edge of a couch. And she was looking again at the magazine he was holding tight in his hands. 'The noise,' he said.

She kept kneading at her thighs with her hands.

'You asked me,' he said. 'You asked me to. And then you slept.' He put the magazine along with the guide in the slot between window and table.

'Oh.' She remembered now. 'So I did. So I did.'

Rain started to beat down – pellets of water hitting the top of the carriage like hoof beats. The sky dimmed.

'My,' Joanie said, taking it all in. 'My-oh-my-oh-my.' She propped her elbows on the table, clasping her hands in a gesture of pleasure. 'Oh! I love the rain when I'm tucked up,' she said.

She kept talking. The rain was so loud that he could not hear what she was saying, but he could see her mouth working.

He counted her face:

eye, eye;

eye, eye, nose.

When the rain eased off a little Joanie settled back in her seat. 'Where are you headed?' she asked. 'Are you going all the way?'

Lately, when he dreams – if he gets to dreaming – vast clouds bank on the horizon. Waves gather, scraping the pitch-black belly of the sky. He wakes, knowing the clouds must spill, the waters must break. Dreaming, he manages to make it all stop, and wait.

Give me time, he asks. Just give me time to work this out.

At home, in the kitchen, he counts the mugs above the sink, and in the bathroom the tiles on the wall. In the hallway, he counts the line of boxes for mail. In the subway, he counts the pillars on the platform, and once on the train he counts the lights that appear in the darkness of the tunnels.

When he counts he tends towards multiples of two, never goes past six. Mostly he sticks to one, two.

Beads of water were being pulled, one by one, backwards, across the window-pane.

'You don't say much,' Joanie said.

They passed an old-fashioned station – lampposts with elegant lampshades, the roof of the building bordered with filigreed woodwork.

'I'm really very easy to get along with,' she said.

They passed a bridge, a criss-cross of girders. They passed a stationary freight train, the wagons a deep green, here and there bursting into blossoms of white graffiti. In the narrow spaces between the wagons he saw, at intervals, a momentary flash of gravel, rail tracks, grass, water, hills, and sky.

'Utica,' said Joanie.

She leant forward, putting both hands flat on the edge of the table, like a contestant in a game show. She held her face in a crush of concentration, and then let it relax.

'Erie!' she said, 'Sandusky!' Her eyes were all lit up. 'I'm guessing where you're going.'

Lately, when he sleeps, he loses his bearings, can't remember where he is: at the hospital, in the chair beside his wife's bed, or alone at home, where he tries to fall asleep on the daybed, watching television, listening to the radio.

When in his dreams he becomes aware of his bladder, he mentally traces two routes to the bathroom before attempting to get to his feet. Route one takes him out of the chair, across the slumbering ward, across the corridor glossed with night lighting, past the nurses' station, past the drinks machine, to the left, or to the right, either one will do. Route two, at home, he kicks the sheet off and pads in his boxers in a beeline. He doesn't need a light. He knows the way. He wipes his hands at the sink – thoroughly – a habit he can't shake, reaching all the while for water, paper towels, antiseptic gel.

The restaurant car's booths had the same blue upholstery as the sleeping compartment. There were groups of people already seated, but the car was not yet full.

'They run a tight ship,' Joanie said. 'You see if they don't.'

A woman seated them – pale, skinny, and drawn. She hovered beside an empty table a moment but then sidestepped to seat them at the one opposite, where a young couple were already deep in their menus, side by side.

'You go,' Joanie said, and he slid on in to take the seat closest to the window. She edged herself down then, on to the end of the couch, beside him. They were facing backwards. He was facing the girl, and Joanie facing the boy. It was an arrangement better suited to old friends, or a double date. The couple didn't acknowledge their arrival at all.

'You ready?' the attendant asked, turning her attention to the couple.

Only the girl looked up. 'Yes,' she said. Her hair was cut in a neat bob. She was maybe in her early twenties.

The attendant waited, pen hanging mid-air over a pad.

'Number twenty-eight,' the girl said. 'Thank you.'

'Both of you?'

'Yes. Thank you,' the girl said, tucking her hair behind her ears; first the right, then the left.

One, two.

The boy was still immersed in the menu.

Sometimes they get muddled – routes one and two – sometimes he'll be halfway to the hospital bathroom and he'll panic, believing, suddenly, that he is in his boxers, for all the world to see, or maybe, worse, his fly is unbuttoned, or maybe, worse still, he has a hard-on. It is not possible, of course. He never falls asleep in the chair beside her bed dressed only in his boxers, and even at home, alone, it is a long while since he has woken up hard. Some switch has flipped. He's not even sorry.

'No drinks?' the attendant asked.

'Can we have water?' the girl said.

'You can have water.' The attendant's hand hovered over the pad as she cast a glance at the boy. 'Both of you?' she asked. The boy didn't move, didn't acknowledge her at all.

'Please. Thanks,' the girl said. She tucked her hair behind her right ear; once, twice. It was just the gesture. There was no hair needing to be tucked.

The attendant shifted her feet side to side as she ticked off the boxes on her sheet. 'You sleeper or coach?' she asked.

'Sleeper,' the girl said.

'Number?'

'Nine.'

'Car?'

'4911.'

'Both of you?'

'Yes,' the girl said.

The only other thing to say about routes one and two is this: he cares about them inasmuch as they get him from here to there, from bladder-full to bladder-empty. These are essentials. Energy expended on anything else is wasted. In the versions he imagines, asleep, as in the versions when he is awake, he walks with tunnel-vision – everything else, everything around the edges, he shuts out.

'I need you to sign,' the attendant said.

She leant forward and handed one sheet to the girl and put another one down on the table with the pen in front of the boy. 'Both of you,' she said. The boy didn't look up. He tilted his head towards the girl, who nodded and pointed at the bottom of the sheet. He took up the pen now. When he was done the girl signed hers and took both sheets and handed them back.

The attendant tore the customer copies from her own copies, deposited them on the table, and left.

At the hospital, he shuts out the other patients, the nurses, their sympathetic smiles, their chat. He shuts out the people who mill around by the drinks machine, and those sitting on the endless rows of plastic chairs.

At home, he shuts out the postcards they have been sent by friends, family, that over time they have stuck to the cupboard above the sink. He shuts out the picture that she painted, badly, in Corsica – rocks, sea, sky – that he had framed and hung in the middle of their living-room wall. He shuts out all the bits and pieces they found together on day trips, museum trips, foreign trips.

From the restaurant car, with windows on both sides, facing backwards, he could see the whole panorama. On his right, the river; on his left, salt-marsh, weatherboard houses, porches bearing the ubiquitous national flag.

The menu was a yellow oblong. Non-Egg Entrée, he read. Egg Substitute. Dinner Special. The list of numbers ran to seventy-nine, but some of the numbers did not have options alongside. He wondered what would happen if you ordered thirty-one when there was no option listed.

'Grits. Oh my,' Joanie said. 'I have not had grits since . . . I don't know when.'

He was watching the couple opposite. He kept expecting one of them to make eye contact, to say something, but neither of them did.

At home he shuts out things other people wouldn't see if they walked with him on his short route: her reading on the daybed with a look of the deepest, most peaceful concentration; or banging pots together in their kitchen in the morning to wake him up; or in the bath sloshing the water, chattering – him, stationed on the toilet lid close by, elbows on knees, eyes on her, listening. No. They wouldn't see any of that. He would rather not see it himself. He shuts it out.

'Where are you all from?' Joanie asked.

The girl gave Joanie a wary smile that did not extend to her eyes. The boy no longer had a menu, but kept his gaze down nonetheless.

'DC,' the girl said.

'Do you like it?' Joanie asked. 'Have you always lived there?'

'We like it,' the girl said. 'Not always. No.'

'Where are you from originally?'

'Michigan.'

'What about you?' Joanie asked the boy, but still he didn't look up.

The girl nudged the boy's hand gently where it lay on the tabletop, and he did look up, a question in his eyes, his head turned to her. The girl leant in and said right into his ear, 'Where are you from, the lady is asking.' He frowned, moved closer, studying her lips, as if all the answers were there. She tried again, gesturing at Joanie, and finally then he took their companions in.

'I don't hear well,' he said, loudly, so that people nearby were twisting in their seats to look. There was a small distortion in the way he spoke, but the words were clear.

He turned back to the girl then. He nodded, very slightly, just once.

She did the same. And she smiled at him.

It was the briefest exchange.

The sleeping ward, early that morning, had brought him back to night flights they had taken together. Cabin lights off and shutters down. Air hostesses – attentive like nurses – drifting up the darkened passageways, shadowy moths in the half light, now and then summoned by a lone glow.

He had enjoyed being lodged for those hours in the purring heart of the jet, while beside him his wife, who could never sleep on a plane, talked quietly, non-stop, spinning tales to keep her mind off the fact they were in a tin can, too high, trawling her memory bank for odd fragments, sending a stream of offerings to him through the fuggy cabin air – a picnic in Maine, a school trip to the city, the particular challenge of a long-forgotten ballet pose. Their heads would be resting close, and as he listened he would feel her breath on his ear, across his cheek, his nose.

It was so stealthy, the memory, that it had taken him by surprise. He was tired. His defences were down. He had tried to make it stop, but something had already taken hold – vice-like at the back of his neck, reaching deep into his chest.

He had left the hospital. It was still early. The streets were almost empty.

He walked in Central Park where the trees were black-barked and lacquered in the rain, the ground studded with fragments – foliage frayed and cast down by the wind. He bought coffee at a coffee bar in a mall at Columbus Circle. He walked on south towards the glint and flare of lights in Times Square, which he tracked from several blocks up, great swatches of colour against the buildings, pulsing towards the leached sky.

At Madison Square Garden, instead of continuing to his office, he followed the stream of bodies heading for Penn Station.

A normal interaction: something to bring her with him into the world. At Hudson News: a bottle of water and a magazine. A conversation with the woman at the counter.

But as she gave him change – the woman's skin against his.

And then staring at the hoarding for Amtrak, choosing at random, buying a ticket. Waking from his daze on board the Lake Shore Limited.

It was night and they were walking beside the canal. Lamplight played over the water and canal boats sat pretty with plant pots studding their roofs and small boats tethered beside them. The air was warm and flush with a grapey smell of summer. Her hand was closed around his wrist. She liked to feel the beat of his pulse. His arm was around her waist and tucked into the front of her jeans. She could feel her hip-bone against his palm as they walked.

'What are the chances?' he said.

'And then to be sitting there on the plane. Side by side. It's kind of amazing. It *is* amazing. We're so lucky,' she said.

He grinned at her, taking her in as they walked. 'D'you think?' She grinned back.

'Listen to us. So smug. It's funny,' he said.

He stopped walking. 'You're wearing my shirt.' She'd put it on in their room after her shower. 'You *are* amazing.' He raised his voice and called it out, 'AM-AZ-ING!' It echoed, by the canal.

'Shhhh!' She laughed.

'No one can hear. It's the middle of the night.'

'Uh oh,' she said. 'And you could be anyone. We *have* only just met. Joggers find body in local beauty spot. Girl, twenties; last seen at airport with white male, medium build.'

'Er, last seen in hotel with white male, medium build.'

'Silly girl.'

'Yep.'

He bent to pick up stones from the path and then started to throw them towards the other bank. The stones hit the side and fell noisily into the water.

'Hey,' she said.

'No one can hear.'

They had left the lamplight behind and it was hard to see, so he was throwing stones out into the black. She could just make out the ripples coming back from the other side, across the water towards them. She counted the ripples; one, two, three, four.

'Hey. What's that?' she said.

It wasn't a stone. He hadn't just thrown a stone. She was counting ripples from the stone he had thrown before. It wasn't his noise. She listened. It sounded like . . . it sounded like someone chuckling . . . it sounded like someone was nearby and shaking, and chuckling.

It was hard to make anything out. They peered across the water. They looked both ways up and down the canal. They held still and listened for where the sound was coming from.

Nothing. They looked at each other expectantly. She clasped his hand. She laughed, suddenly, breathlessly, as she waited, listening. He looked back at her, silent.

They used their mobile phones for light, casting a blue-grey glow out on to the path in front of them. She thought she saw an otter, or a seal, sleek and wet and fresh from the water, dark eyes looking back at her, right there in front of them where the slope from the road met the path. They stepped closer and suddenly there were legs kicking up dust, frantically pawing the gravel. A dog. A black Labrador trying to move itself along on its side, front legs going fast like it was sleeping and dreaming of running. They moved closer still and it started to whine. They took in the whiteness of bone from its skull and the trail it had left down the bank behind and its coat wet with blood.

It looked as if someone had hit it on the road above and either it had fallen or been pushed over the side. She hoped it hadn't been pushed. She hoped the driver could not have noticed, but knew he must have. The hind legs of the dog had been crushed. It must have been hit hard. It must have been run over and maybe dragged some way.

'Whatever happened you wouldn't just have not noticed,' she said.

This was not a small dog. It would've been like hitting a young deer or something.

She turned away from the dog and let the light on her phone fade. He switched his off then and they were in darkness again but still she could hear the animal kicking up dust with those front legs.

'What do we do?' she whispered. 'Should we move it? Could we take it somewhere?'

'It's late. It's night. Where's open?'

'We could ask at the hotel.'

'I don't think we can move it. It's not in a good way.'

'One of us should stay. You go.'

'Where?'

'Find help.'

'I'm not going to leave you here at, what, one in the morning, on your own. It's not safe.'

'Well, I'll go.'

'No. Same reason.'

'We've got to do something.'

'I know.'

The dog had stopped making noises and they flicked on their phones and shone the light down, but it was looking right at them. There was blood and spittle coming from its jaws. It murmured and looked at them.

She looked back, lost for a moment, unable to take her eyes from the dog.

He said, 'I don't know that I can pick it up.'

'I'll help.'

'I don't know that it's possible. Without leaving some of it behind,' he said.

'God.'

'We could try to track down a number for a vet, but we can't exactly call an ambulance for a dog.'

'Don't they have things like that . . . for dogs?' she asked.

'I don't think it would make it anyway,' he said. 'I just don't think it's going to last.'

She looked at him. 'Are you serious? Are you really sure? How do you know?'

'I don't,' he said.

He was thinking of his dad breaking a duckling's neck when they were living on the farm. The boy who was his friend at the time had been running too fast and trodden on this duckling and damaged it too badly for it to survive. He did not think he was strong enough to break the dog's neck.

'It's in a lot of pain,' he said. 'And it would have to be moved. I think moving it would kill it anyway.'

'Oh.'

'I really think so. And I think it would be cruel.'

She bit her lip.

'I think we have to kill it,' he said.

'Oh. Oh God.' She was trying hard not to cry.

'I think we have to,' he said.

'Can you do it? Do you think you can do it? Because I'm not sure I can.'

'It's okay,' he said. 'I'll do it.'

She nodded. 'Okay.'

He got the light on his phone up and shone it around to find a stone or something to use to kill the dog and found a brick on the grass close by. He moved over to the dog and standing above it, paused.

'Okay,' he said.

He was lifting his arm to strike when he said, 'I'm really very sorry but I'm going to have to ask you to shine the light. I don't think I can do this with one hand.'

She nodded her head in the dark and came over to him and he handed her the phone and as soon as she had both lights on for him to see what he was doing he struck the dog hard on its neck. The dog lurched, but its legs started up again, scrabbling in the dirt. 'Shit,' he said. She heard him take a deep breath and then he brought the brick down again, this time on the skull. The dog whimpered. He brought the brick down a third time. Something crunched beneath it. Not dead.

'Maybe you should stop,' she said. 'Maybe it's okay. Maybe it's not as bad as it looks.'

'Christ,' he said.

'What do you mean? Don't you agree? It's not dying.'

'I know,' he said. He sounded disgusted.

'Why are you angry with me?' she asked.

'I'm not angry with you. I just can't stop now. I can't stop it now.'

'Why?'

'I can't. I've hit it. I've hit it with the brick.'

'So you're going to give up?'

'I'm not giving up on it. I'm going to kill it.'

She made a sound that got lodged in her throat.

'Unless you want to take over?'

She shook her head.

'Can you shine the phones again, please.' It was spoken flatly, plainly, like a surgeon asking her to pass the scalpel mid-operation.

She held the phones side by side and shone their beams down. She tried to make the noise into something else in her head to stop her stomach lurching. She could not turn far enough away to shut out the sight of it as she held the phones and she could not make the noise into something else.

There was a sharp crack and then, 'It's dead. Whatever. It's dead.'

'Sure?'

'I broke its neck. I used my hands and my foot and I broke its neck. It's dead.'

'Good.'

'Yep.'

'Should we bury it?'

'You bury it. I'm done.'

He washed his hands in the canal.

They walked in silence back along the towpath. There was electricity between their arms as they walked, side by side. She felt herself flinching, anticipating his arm brushing against hers. She still held both of their phones – one in each hand. She held on to them as if they might steady her as she walked.

She let them into the hotel and he took his trainers off at the door and they crept up the stairs and to the room without anyone seeing them. She put the kettle on for something to do as he shut himself in the bathroom and turned the taps on for a bath. She made hot chocolate from one of the little sachets in the basket by the kettle and added sugar, packet after packet. She made him a coffee. She didn't know if he took sugar but she laid out a neat row of packets by his cup, and she put a spoon in the saucer for him to stir it in with, if he used it. She sat down on the bed and waited, looking at the cups on the table in front of her.

He started whistling. He was in the bath because she heard the water being splashed, and he started whistling. He was whistling too hard. She knew he wanted her to hear him. Whistling. She sat frozen on the end of the bed looking at the door to the bathroom. She felt she needed to swallow. She felt something stuck in her throat but she couldn't swallow.

He had taken the plug out of the bath and she could hear him padding around and fiddling and whistling.

She forced herself to stand, and then got rooted at the edge of the bed. She looked over to her side where the clothes she had worn on the flight lay in a heap. She remembered she was wearing his shirt.

He opened the door of the bathroom and a cloud of misty air came into the bedroom and he smiled at her. 'Ready?'

She was standing there in her bra, holding his shirt out. He came towards her with his fingers pink from the bath and took it from her.

'We were going to eat remember?' he said. 'Still want to?'

She didn't reply. She looked past him. She listened to the murmur of the fan coming from the bathroom. She looked to where the bath mat sat crumpled on the wet floor. She saw his trainers in the corner by the sink.

'Where are the numbers for takeaway?' he asked.

He came close to her and reached for her and she froze as his arms went around her.

'Don't touch me,' she said.

She pulled away from him and went to the wardrobe for her suitcase and then planted it on the bed. She went to the bathroom and took her toothbrush and her wash bag and her make-up. Her face was odd and blotchy in the mirror.

'What are you doing?' he asked. 'What's going on?'

She came back to the bedroom and tucked the wash bag and the make-up in her case, then put the clothes from the bed on top and zipped it shut. She took a top that she'd hung in the wardrobe and put it on. She lifted the case from the bed and put it on the floor, pulling the handle up and out so that she could wheel it along.

'What are you doing?' he asked again. He was standing there looking confused. Just standing there, holding his shirt.

She grasped the handle of her case. She thought how strange he seemed and how odd it was that they'd slept together just a few hours before. It was amazing.

She knew she looked terrible and she realised she liked it. She was in love with the puffiness of her face and the rage that was tingeing it red.

'I have to go now,' she said, flatly.

He stood there. He didn't say anything.

She left the room and went downstairs and out of the hotel. She crossed the street and made her way back along the route they had followed. She took the path down to the canal. She saw the lamplight casting shadows from the street. She saw the plant pots and the tethered boats. She felt the gravel on the path crunching gently beneath her until she reached the edge of the water. She set her case, handle in. Using one hand to support herself she sat down on the broad stones that paved the side of the path. Her feet dangled. It was getting cold. She adjusted her legs so that she was comfortable and sat still, listening to the water lapping at the side of the canal.

DISAPPEARANCES

The beginning is simple enough: I find myself in the park due to a sudden and overwhelming urge to go to the museum.

People speak of the shock of retirement. They warn of the possibility of profound depression. However, this is not something I expect for myself. The life I have built here over the years keeps me more than occupied, regardless of work. And so it comes as a surprise to me – this nervous and shifty feeling on waking. It is as if I can only sidle up to the day, like a neurotic suitor.

My restlessness increasingly translates itself into abrupt impulses. To put it bluntly, an urge presents itself much in the manner of the need to urinate or defecate, and demanding immediate action. It is due to just such an impulse that I find myself on the steps of the museum at an absurdly early hour without any real justification for being there.

The museum – established many years ago, and in part with my family's money – houses a moderate collection of European art, mostly paintings, some sculpture, in a building of national importance warranting both attention and preservation. It is a while since I've been there. Not since '93 perhaps.

It is closed, of course. Everywhere is closed at this time of day.

I consider my options. I could return to the apartment. Carolina will be there soon enough to make my coffee and breakfast. However I have woken to a clear sky and it remains fine. It has been neither a long walk nor an unpleasant one, passing through the park. Under the circumstances I decide to walk on.

The jacarandas are coming into bloom. It is spring – and early enough in the day to find some moments of peace before the city's traffic starts spewing noise and fumes.

I find myself gravitating to the edge of the park in the hope of locating a newspaper stand before heading for home.

It is odd how places local to us can remain invisible for so long – until one day they simply present themselves.

The café sits directly on the corner of what is, by day, a busy avenue. It is set back however, separated by railings, a broad curve of paving stones, and the beginnings of a long colonnade.

I cross the avenue and look in. I see a mahogany bar and small, round tabletops. There is no one in sight.

I try the door; it opens. I enter, and take a seat.

From my table I can see the park opposite, with its careful beds of colour, its gravelled paths and ornamental fountains.

As I wait, I watch light enter through the deco windows

that overlook the colonnade. I watch greens and reds and blues from the stained glass play across the black and white tiling on the floor. They meddle with its orderly geometry.

I glance up and see a woman standing behind the bar. I have not been aware of her. She wears a pressed white shirt, a long black apron tied tight about her waist.

Cafecito, por favor.

When she serves me I notice her hands.

*

It becomes a habit. I spend every morning at the café, at the same table, served always by the same woman. She is the only person working there at this hour.

I wake myself up every day at five. It becomes automatic, no need for an alarm. I throw on clothes, and head out. I stroll in the park – without fail I go to the museum. I stand on the steps, look up at the door – it is always closed, the museum always shut. I observe the building for a few moments, and walk on. I trace my path beside the row of jacarandas.

At the edge of the park I cross the avenue. I look through the window of the café before entering and sitting in my usual spot.

The first morning I order my coffee in Spanish and every morning afterwards I do the same. This is unusual. Both in my line of work and in my social life I have been most used to speaking English – other than for that period at the start of the eighties. I was schooled in England and trained for my profession there, so the language is habitual. It would be accurate to say that by and large I reserve the use of Spanish for communication with Carolina, and other help.

I might also mention that the clothes I am wearing on the first day I continue to wear every day, at this hour. I dress in haste – and while I do not quite head out in night attire the general effect cannot be far off. I am not one given to wearing sporting clothes outside the home, but a tracksuit is near enough the truth. I look as though I might have been speed-walking, for health. Suffice to say that according to my usual standards I am unrecognisable.

Now, therefore, I find myself each day close to home, in my neighbourhood, but at an hour when no one I know is about. I do not look as I usually would. I do not speak as I usually do.

The moment anyone else enters the café, I leave.

The rest of my day continues as before. I go home. I shower. I change into something more appropriate. Carolina has my breakfast prepared, as ever. I spend the day in social engagements.

I have spoken of my retirement as something unnerving, but I am not to be pitied. I live in the city's most expensive district. My work introduced me to the wealthiest and most beautiful of Buenos Aires. I made them more beautiful under my knife; they made me wealthier. I was adopted into their circle, popular for my skills as a surgeon, but also for a family history woven through the streets in plaques and memorials: a flawless pedigree.

It is in truth quite some time since I've paid much attention to family. As a young man in the fifties, I longed to be rid of the burden of their decency. I could not bear the thought of following their traditions, their moral imperatives, faithfully treading the path of generations like a mule. I had inherited a good mind, and after some years of training in Oxford, England, I qualified as a surgeon, only to turn my hand to facelifts. I considered myself very clever indeed. I believe I was in pursuit of something perverse – the more vulgar the better. I returned to Buenos Aires and set up shop on home turf to make an exhibition of myself. The family were appalled of course, and I stopped seeing them.

It was a game. I took pleasure in playing the subversive. It suited me well.

The waitress asks me what I do for a living.

I laugh. I'm an old man. I'm retired.

She persists. She wants to know.

This is not a conversation I want to have. I enjoy being a stranger. I like this woman knowing nothing of my life, or who I am. I would like to keep it that way.

But it's the first sign of interest she has shown me, and it would be rude not to respond. Our relationship until now – though largely mute – has been a thing of pleasure. It's hard to explain.

I pause before speaking. I can say anything. I can say I was a poet. I was a road sweeper. I was a baker. I was an architect. She'll never know.

I thrived. It didn't matter who was in charge – throughout the decades, through all the ins and outs, the various shenanigans our country went through. While the leadership had wives and mistresses I was in demand. And while I have never possessed matinée idol looks, I flatter myself that I was their Hephaestus – these women love being done by an ugly man if he is craftsman to the gods.

I tell her I was a surgeon. I am not more specific than that.

I think it will end there, our chat, but she interprets what I say – she assumes I was a general surgeon, and goes on to tell me about the man who saved her brother's life when she was eight, at the time her father disappeared. Of course, not everyone has had my easy run through the years.

Her eyes are warm as she relates this tale, nonetheless. She even takes a seat on the chair across from mine. When she has finished – the story is not long, but quite moving – she studies me in open admiration.

I know that I can end it there and then. A couple of words would suffice. But I don't.

She holds out her hand and shakes mine, solemnly – as if we have some pact – before standing, putting the chair back in position, and resuming work.

I remain at my table. I finish my coffee. I retain the sensation of the smooth swell of scar tissue I felt against my palm as she took my hand. Not burns as I had first thought, but what must have been deep lacerations, horizontal, on both of her palms.

I think to myself, again, what does it matter? What does it matter what she thinks I did, the sort of man she imagines I have been.

When I get up to leave she stops what she's doing and smiles at me from behind the bar.

I'm Beatriz, she says.

I maintain the illusion she's created. It's not hard. If she likes thinking of me as some sort of hero, should I stop her? I like these mornings, and am loath to disrupt them. I like the silent agreement, the way she mostly ignores me, works around me. And she obviously admires the work she thinks I have done.

Our mornings continue. The days are warm. The jacarandas bloom like fists unfurling underneath clear skies.

Irene Varela-Morales. She is an acquaintance – in her fifties. She doesn't see me sitting in the corner, and I have no particular wish to be seen.

I gave her a noble nose. It improved things immeasurably and she's well aware of it. She carries herself in such a way that her profile is always seen to full advantage.

Irene stands impatiently – though making sure she's side-on to the approaching waitress – unwilling, it seems, either to take a seat or stand by the bar. There is a brief exchange – she doesn't look at my Beatriz – and then she takes a table near the door. She faces away from the bar, towards the street.

Beatriz leaves to fulfil the order she has been given but is called back. Irene stands, and – visibly irritated, still side-on, without looking at Beatriz – casts her wrap across the table, into her face, with great force. Such is her surprise, and the speed with which it is slung, that it is all Beatriz can do to catch the thing before it slips to the floor.

She takes it, smooths it, hangs it on the stand beside the door. Irene could have done it herself. The stand is right there.

Beatriz says nothing. She returns to the bar.

Soon she is back at the table, putting down a coffee, milk and water, with a plate of *medialunas*.

The moment she has gone Irene calls her back. She speaks in English with a phoney American drawl. She says, 'I don't want that,' of the *medialunas*, and 'I asked for hot milk. Take this back.'

Beatriz doesn't answer. She looks at the jug that Irene's holding out. '*Leche. Caliente*,' Irene says slowly.

Beatriz goes back to the bar and, moments later, returns with another jug.

'It really shouldn't be this complicated,' Irene says. She speaks first in English and then follows it with Spanish.

She plays this game a good while.

More water.

Ice.

Another spoon.

A clean one.

Beatriz adjusts the awning over the windows, outside – the sun is in Irene's eyes.

When she departs, she doesn't leave a tip.

It is true that the people can be rude here in Recoleta, where there is so much money. The very wealthy too often forget their manners – maybe because they have no cause to remember them. Often they give the impression that it is not forgetfulness at all but clear intention that makes them do it, a kind of assertion of their greater importance in the world; a ruse of sorts that often works – at the very least, superficially.

I see it in Beatriz's face.

It is true that many of them are my neighbours – these people are the sort of people I have known, my friends, even; though I have had no reason to discuss this with her. We have set the parameters of our acquaintance.

She pulls out the chair that sits across from me a second time. She lights a cigarette.

'When they want to take their time, they take their time,' she says. 'When they want to get out of here quickly, they do. They want what they want and they make it known. "This is what I want. This is not what I want. What is this? This is *not* what I ordered. Get the manager – my maid called to reserve and this idiot didn't write it down." These people – they throw their money at you. They never look you in the eye. They like to assume that you are stupid. Maybe it's more fun that way.'

She shrugs. She stubs out her cigarette, and then she gives me that smile. 'These people,' she says.

I don't know how to respond. I reach across the table to take a sip of coffee but somehow – my hand is trembling, it's been happening of late – I spill it. 'Stupid,' I say. 'I'm so sorry.'

'They have been working hard, these hands. Give them a break,' she says.

She takes my hand between her palms.

I cannot remember whether my acquaintance with Irene was simply professional, or more.

I have been acquainted with a number of women. The term 'acquaintance' is undoubtedly correct. I have not been one for long alliances.

I was married – once – an odd, abortive affair.

I have been so used to unravelling women, peeling back their faces, constantly imagining them into something other than they are.

It is not that I have not enjoyed them – far from it – but they are no more or less than the sum of their parts.

It's natural.

Irene Varela-Morales returns to the café. She brings a friend, Valentina – I forget, but I think the surname is Suarez.

They assault my table.

'I told you he was hiding out in this place.'

She claims she spotted me from the first – *knew* she recognised me, but couldn't place me in those *ghastly* clothes.

Valentina launches herself. 'Look at you! I can't *believe* you thought you'd get away with it!'

'What a bad, bad, naughty boy,' adds Irene.

Impossible to pretend that I don't know them, that they've made a mistake. I'm just not quick enough off the mark. It's far too complicated to attempt.

They seat themselves. Beatriz approaches. I try not to say more than I need, although the damage is done.

They order in English. I order another coffee, in Spanish.

She walks away. I watch her shoulders become small, like those of a child.

The conversation develops. I try to resist the talk of mutual acquaintances but can't for long. Impossible to sit there and say nothing.

They talk loudly these women. They dominate any space they are in. It's their way. If Beatriz were hiding in the kitchen she would hear every word.

'So, Alfredo Martinez is dead.'

'Not before time.'

'*Irene!* Terrible!' Valentina snorts.

'Come on, but it's true. He was ancient. They absolutely *stuffed* him for the coffin. He'd lost a *lot* of weight.'

'And such a handsome man once. He really could have done with some work before such a public display.'

'*Mean* of you not to offer, Julio Ortiz. A gentleman like you.'

'I'm no longer able, as perhaps you know – my hands,' I say. 'And it's not yet *standard* practice to offer a facelift to a corpse.'

'You can do me any day,' Irene drawls. 'Dead or alive.'

'Me too!' Valentina adds.

'But what about your hands? Don't you try to tell me that they've lost their touch.'

'Irene.'

'Now, don't be coy. We all know who has the magician's fingers in BA!'

They laugh together. They are in fits at this smut.

I can't help it; I am chuckling too.

They leave ahead of me, with promises of drinks, very soon, from all of us.

I linger on in the café, not sure what it is that I am waiting for. Beatriz has left the bill on the table. There is no further need for her to appear. I know she will not.

I take out my wallet and rifle for notes. My hand is shaking, yet again, and I drop it on the floor.

I have to get down on my knees. I gather up the notes that have fallen, pick up my wallet and, overheated, sit back in my chair.

I am still clasping a handful of notes. I put them away, and leave the precise amount on the bill, no more, no less, in small change.

I walk away from my table and out of the door, without looking back. I feel profound melancholy. The door swings shut.

*

Pay attention. This is important.

She is not beautiful. Her face is not symmetrical. As a rule of thumb beauty requires symmetry and, as with so many people, the two sides of her face don't match.

Her left eye opens wider than her right – when she is tired her right eye can look half closed. In fact, there is a kind of heaviness to the right side of her face, as if it were somehow more susceptible – to what . . . gravity, grief?

Her lower lip is larger than her upper, and there is a jaggedness to the outline of the upper that is at odds with the whole. She has a dimple that is stretching to a deep line on her right cheek.

A smoker. Indeed, we have smoked together. It is a passion we share. I know, regardless, that she has smoked for some years, from the traces of lines on her upper lip; again, on the right.

Her left-hand side is something else. Her eye is bright and alert, a sense of humour always close at hand. She has green eyes, I may not have mentioned. Whereas on the right the lines that cluster around her eye add age and some sadness, on the left they appear to bear witness to laughter, *joie de vivre*.

She has a minimal cleft in her chin – almost another dimple – which lends her face strength overall.

When she smokes, she plants the cigarette between her teeth, in the very centre, as she lights it. Her first drag then is forthright, determined, before the cigarette wanders off to the right and hangs loosely, as if it might drop from her lips.

She has dark hair. It is of medium length, and most often tied back.

She is moderately tall.

She is – to hazard a guess, taking into account the puffiness beneath the eyes, the lines now visible on her forehead, the loss of youthful volume in her lips – in her late thirties.

She has a small waist. She has scarred hands.

THE HUMAN CIRCADIAN PACEMAKER

Her first glimpse of him, he was walking towards her lurching from side to side like a drunk. She flung her arms around him.

'How are you?' she said.

A lopsided smile. 'I'm A-OK.'

'So what have you been up to?'

'Stuff,' he said. 'You?'

'Oh, stuff.'

They didn't get to talk very much at first, there was so much going on. She went back home; he stayed on for medical assessments, press conferences.

For the champagne reception she wore a dress that she had bought for the occasion. Putting it on she felt strangely like a schoolgirl going on a date. She didn't know what he would be like now, when so much had happened to him. Before going out she threw a wrap over her shoulders and then hugged herself in front of the mirror. He hadn't been home yet. Everything looked as it had for the last few months.

She had been warned, of course. Partners, spouses, went through training as well. They were told to expect change. They were warned about the psychological, the physiological. As they sat there on their chairs together in that room they had exchanged tentative smiles. Oh my goodness, their smiles said. What have we gotten ourselves into?

Sometimes at night she would lie in bed and run through the changes they had been told about and imagine the most extreme scenarios and be afraid. She would worry that he would come back with another man's face.

Arriving at the reception she waited for him to notice her standing on the parquet in her new dress, and he did notice her, and he walked over with his new rolling gait and he held on to her upper arms tightly with his hands and looked at her.

'Hey,' she said.

'Hey yourself.'

His eyes were full of light. He looked giddy.

'Stay right where you are,' he said.

She watched him cross the floor to the long table where they were serving drinks. He collected two glasses of champagne, put them down to shake hands with the bartender, who looked pretty happy himself, picked them up again, wheeled around, and made his way back to her. He was finding his sea legs, walking on a shifting deck.

They had been warned about difficulties with balance, about lack of coordination between hand, eye and head, and she was glad they had been prepared, but annoyed now that she found herself watching him so closely, watching for the signs. It doesn't matter, she reminded herself. It won't last.

'You walk like a drunk,' she said, when he arrived, toppling, in front of her. He leant towards her. She thought he was going to kiss her but he didn't. He raised the two glasses of champagne and looked at her over the small golden explosions.

She took her glass and they sipped at their champagne without speaking. It was cold and good. She didn't try to chink glasses: something might go wrong – hand, eye, head.

As the room filled, its constellations shifted between team clusters and family clusters. She watched and was glad that it had gone so well. She couldn't help studying him – every gesture, every expression that passed across his face. Even deep in conversation she listened out for his voice. She weighed him up next to the others. A few of them were hamming it up, staggering about. One was rocking slowly backwards and forwards on the balls of his feet.

There were impromptu speeches, some of them quite silly. The team aired mission jokes which meant little to anyone else. A multitude of looks, smiles, gestures passed back and forth between them. Sometimes just glancing at each other would set them off.

In the faces of the other wives she recognised her own bewilderment.

They left the party about eleven; they were sent home, the team, like they were still in high school. They were told to get a good night's rest. Everyone shook hands. There were sparks of laughter. Manly hugs. Back patting. They all left the room together, everyone grinning and looking tired.

She drove home. He sat in the passenger seat across from her, his head lolling as they hit the dirt road; otherwise still, eyes shut.

The night was clear and she thought you must be able to see all of the stars. She wanted to pull over and get out of the car. She wanted to ask him – out in the middle of nowhere, by themselves – what it was like up there.

Tell me, she wanted to say, now that you're back – does space really smell like rubber? They say it does.

She thought about putting the radio on, but was worried the noise would wake him. Instead, steering with one hand, she wound down the window and pulled out her pack of cigarettes. When she had one lit she looked across at him, and then kept glancing back, every few seconds, all the way home.

They had been warned about accelerated aging: cardiovascular decline, and muscle atrophy, and weakened bones. None of them looked any older, but inside things had changed.

The human circadian pacemaker had undergone change: they had been warned too about disruptions to sleep. His rhythms were all off. His body clock was shot.

She woke to find him gone from their bed and there he was, sitting in the kitchen, three in the morning, looking at his hands.

'Okay?' she asked.

He looked up, but said nothing. She had the odd sensation that he didn't recognise her at all.

Before the mission the astronauts had used bright light to adjust for the flight, to help reset the body clock.

She had got a light box for his return. She had put it in the corner of their room, experimented with levels. At the highest it emitted a shock of bright white light that made her squint.

She pulled out a chair and sat across from him with a book. She had started it that week – though with the excitement of his return hadn't made much progress.

Now, under the disc of light cast by the lamp above them, she read.

At some point he got up and left the room. He got out of his chair so slowly she barely registered the movement. He walked like an old man. She moved to help but he waved her away, he said, 'I have to do this myself.' So she watched until he reached the doorway and turned to go upstairs, and then listened as he made his way one step at a time to the top.

She continued to read, as if the act, so far through the night and into the morning, were a way of keeping him company as he suffered under gravity.

They had regimes to keep them in shape. There were exercises to help maintain a basic level of health. The mission had been a long one though, and under the conditions there were limits to what a man could do. There were limits also to what he could control – certain things just happened. He had sent her a photo of himself with his 'space face'. He was all puffed up, they told her, due to a movement of fluids with the loss of gravity.

The night before launch he had been at the base. She had tried to sleep, but failed, and got up early. She opened the curtains and looked up at the sky, which was a perfect blue, just as it should be. She remembered a feeling of sawdust in her eyes, the sense she wasn't quite in her body.

So long as I don't have to talk to anyone, she had thought. So long as I don't have to open my mouth.

When she got home she had gone straight to bed though it was still early. Lying on her side, she brought her knees up close to her chest and then wrapped one arm around them to pull them closer still. She tucked her other arm underneath the pillow. There her fingers found a packet of freeze-dried Neapolitan ice-cream. On the front, an image of a rocket launching into space; above it the words SPACE FOOD. She had started laughing, and then she had found that she was crying instead.

With only one packet, she had been superstitious about using it. For weeks she carried it around like a charm. If she left the house without it she would go back and start her journey over. In time she discovered he'd hidden packets all over the place – slipped into socks in her underwear drawer, stowed inside DVD cases – so she no longer felt she always had to carry it around, and actually, finally, opened a packet to try it out. The taste wasn't bad, though the consistency was wrong. She wondered if this really was the stuff they had up there. She imagined them all opening and mixing their packets, discussing the flavours. There was something about it that made her laugh, the idea of them tearing open these things marked SPACE FOOD, as if they might go astray and eat the wrong kind of food without that heading in bold type to keep things clear.

She found no way to make space familiar, beyond this. She couldn't get past something imagined from childhood – tin cans; the Clangers; egg-boxes with antennae made of flexible straws.

Upstairs, in their bedroom, the light box was brightening in the corner. It was domed, sun-like and set to progress through a simulated sunrise. He was balled up hidden beneath the duvet. She sat on the edge of the bed with his coffee in her hand and watched the light shift from red through orange to white.

She had met him at an aerodrome in Texas. She was visiting a friend who was studying out there and who was considering taking flying lessons. They had gone along to watch the training planes take off and land, over and over, on the thin strip of tarmac in the middle of all that dry earth. They sat in the heat drinking Coke, trying to make out faces in the stream of tiny planes. Each touched down for a moment only before taking off and looping around again. It was hypnotic enough and they were lazy enough to sit there until the circuits were over and the pilots and pupils came in and debriefed.

She had gone inside the hangar to use the toilet and was on her way out when she bumped into him. She was wiping her hands on her jeans, not looking where she was going. She recognised him as one of the pilots, and told him about her friend, and he had come to join them for a beer.

The three of them sat there until dark. Small planes appeared intermittently up above, lights winking like fireflies before touching down.

Late on, when her friend had gone inside, and they found themselves suddenly alone, something happened, there was an exchange of some sort, and awareness crept to the surface as they spoke, sitting there on aluminium chairs, their forearms resting on the cool tabletop.

He had come around, and stood behind her chair, lightly touched the back of her neck.

*

'I feel like shit,' he announced brightly, walking into the kitchen late morning, his eyes puffed up, blinking. 'I keep bumping into things,' he said. 'I hit my shin.' He showed her his leg. It was bleeding. Still, he was smiling.

'God,' she said. She took him in.

He asked for Marmite on toast. For someone who thought Marmite was a big joke he ate a lot of it. Her mother sent it over in packages from England. She hadn't told her that every-thing, now, you could get in the States. She liked receiving packages from her mother.

She asked him how long it would take for his body to adapt and he said he didn't know. Some people adapt back quickly; some don't.

'I'm fit and healthy,' he said. To prove it, he fastened his hands on the doorframe, pulled himself up, hung for a moment, grinned at her, and then dropped. 'I'm fine. Watch me.' He moved from the doorway one foot in front of the other, arms out at either side, eyes fixed on her. Midway across the room he toppled and then lurched, catching his hip on the table. Things flew. Milk dripped on to the floor.

He surveyed the damage with an expression of total neutrality, and returned to his tightrope.

'Sit down, why don't you?' she said. 'Just a thought.'

He was concentrating on his feet.

Your leg. Fresh blood was welling up. She watched it bead, trace a route south.

'Did you notice my hair?' he asked. 'I didn't wash it once.' His hair was glossy, healthy. 'SPACE HAIR,' he said.

'Would a bath be a good thing?'

He spent the rest of the morning walking slowly around the house, patrolling the garden, sitting on the porch. She found it hard not to follow him.

It was as if he had just got his sight back, the way he was looking at everything.

*

For a couple of weeks they were supposed to keep in touch with the base, stay local, though mornings were officially his own, and some afternoons might pan out that way too. The initial surge of activity was over.

At lunch-time he said, 'I'm going to meet the guys.' It was a statement. There was no suggestion that she should come along but she didn't stop to think about that.

'Just give me a second,' she said.

She found herself tucked in at a table with the team, dipping chicken wings and fries into ketchup and mayonnaise, alternating tumblers of Sprite with bottles of beer, listening as they recounted the food they missed the most up there. She was the only wife who had come along.

Corpse she knew well, and Shrink Fit, through reputation. Elvis and Gandalf and Steve Buscemi she had met only briefly, though she had absorbed the stories about them all. Originally a woman had been set for their mission, but she had to pull out.

'Oreos,' Elvis said.

'No,' said Gandalf. 'Someone always says Oreos. Can we get some more ketchup here?' He gesticulated to the waitress with the visual aid of the empty bottle, put it back on the table in front of him, and, looking circumspect, rotated it in the palms of his hands. 'I hate the crust,' he said. 'Do you see the crust on that?' He held the bottle up so that everyone could get a proper look at the rim.

'Hey. Why don't you pass it round?' Steve B said.

'Hey. Why don't they do something about the crust?' said Gandalf.

'It's not the crust that bothers me,' Shrink Fit said. 'It's that watery shit at the bottom.'

She glanced at him, sitting at the end of the table, hands behind his head, legs outstretched. He wasn't saying anything, but he looked happy enough, just soaking it up. These are my guys, his look seemed to be saying. It's all good.

'I get to choose,' Elvis said. 'It's my food.'

'It's everyone's food. You can't say Oreos, man.' Shrink Fit reached for a fry, shaking his head slowly, as if at some profound truth.

'Whose rules are these?' Elvis said. 'This is bullshit.' He punctuated what seemed to be a genuine frustration with a chicken wing that had never quite made it to his mouth.

'Christ. Are we still on the fucking Oreos?' Gandalf asked.

'You just can't say Oreos,' Shrink Fit said again.

'Motherfucker,' said Elvis.

The waitress brought a new bottle of ketchup and set it in the middle of the table.

'Can I give you this? I hate looking at the crust.' Gandalf handed her the empty bottle, ignoring the look she gave him in return.

'The thing is,' he turned his attention to the table. 'And this is fundamental.' He set his hands palms down, as if laying down the law. 'You *get* the Oreos. Everyone gets the Oreos. It's a given. You get those for free. So you get to choose something else.' He gave Elvis a rictus smile. 'This is how you should think of it.'

'I don't see the problem with this,' Steve B said. 'Everyone's happy, right?'

'Everyone's happy.' Shrink Fit beat out a rhythm on the table top, grinning to himself.

She got up from the table, prompting a ripple of tut-tutting as she walked towards the door.

She was leaning forward, cupping her cigarette, trying to light it in the breeze, when she felt a pair of hands on her shoulders.

'El-ea-nor.' It was Corpse. 'Save me from these assholes.'

She smiled. He had always called her that, punishing her accent with a kind of mock-respect, as if she were royalty. The only other people who used her full name were her parents.

Facing her then, he held her at arm's length and looked her up and down. He was a man who had never stopped looking like a teen, long-limbed and gangly. In the bright, clear sunlight he appeared paler than ever – skin translucent, eyelashes near invisible. Even his freckles seemed to have faded.

'How's my girl?' he said, studying her.

'Yeah,' she said, with a nod.

'Stick out your tongue, say "Ah",' he said.

'Ah,' she said.

'Fit as a fiddle. Right as rain,' he said.

He helped her light her cigarette and then lit one for himself, and they stood there together, looking out into the street, smoking and saying nothing. She watched the dust getting picked up in gusts at the side of the road and whirled in circles around and around, like miniature cyclones. The sky was a cold blue, with vague wisps of cloud which seemed to her entirely static, seemed somehow to be grafted on up there.

She surprised herself by letting out a long, low sigh.

Corpse reached across and took her free hand in his. Their palms sat warm against each other. He leant back against the wall of the diner, and she did the same, and he closed his eyes, and she did the same, and together they felt the warmth of the sun on their skin.

'God, that's good,' he said.

The alcohol went straight to all their heads. By late afternoon the astronauts were heading home for bed, tired out and fractious, like small boys.

He allowed her to help him up the stairs, and under the sheets, and then he was out.

*

He was awake in the night. She heard him banging around downstairs. Lying there in bed she tried to follow his movements in her mind. From the amount of noise she imagined a mess. When she woke up in the morning he was fast asleep beside her, and when she went down everything was clean, stowed.

She made toast, and walked in circles around the table in the kitchen, looking for some clue to what he'd done. Moving to the living room she traced her rotations around the edge of the carpet in the middle of the floor. It was bright, patterned, ugly; a wedding gift from one of his friends.

Late morning she tried to coax him out of sleep. She tickled his feet, his ribs. She sprinkled water on his face. She opened the window and let in fresh air. She pulled off the duvet and left it in a heap on the floor. She brought the light box from its place in the corner, held it to his face, and then gave up and just watched him breathe.

She wondered about calling one of the other wives. Instead, while he was sleeping, she tried to concentrate on her work.

When she had moved to the States she had continued working freelance, writing articles on anything that came her way. It had taken a while back home to build up a list that led to steady work – she'd been afraid to start over, but so far, touch wood, things had worked out.

She had to finish a piece on ecological housing. She sat on the bed with the laptop on her knees. As he slept on, she immersed herself in the odd beauty of homes made of earth and tyres, recycled bottles and aluminium cans. Come lunchtime she moved to the porch, and stayed until dusk, her notes spread along the weathered boards.

She woke the next day to find a row of refuse sacks in the hall. As she sat with his coffee on the edge of their bed he was smiling in his sleep.

'A spring clean?' she asked when he appeared downstairs. He looked confused. 'What's in the bags?' she said.

'Just stuff.'

'Like what?'

He shrugged, dismissive. 'I'm starving,' he said. 'What do we have?'

'I didn't hear anything,' she said.

He had the refrigerator door open; was looking in, pensive.

'Hey!' she said.

'Yeah.'

'I didn't hear a thing.'

His hand hovered over something in the fridge and then changed its mind. 'I was quiet as a mouse,' he said.

'You don't have to be. I don't mind. Make all the noise you like.'

'You were asleep.'

'I don't care. Wake me.'

The fridge started whining because the door had been open so long. 'What are you looking for?' she asked.

After breakfast he said he might as well head off to the refuse with those sacks.

'I'll drive you,' she said.

'No need.'

'I'd better drive you,' she said.

They loaded the trunk. At the refuse point she stayed in the car and watched the bags disappear one by one.

She phoned home. 'He finds it hard to talk about,' she told her mother.

'But it must be nice to have him back?'

'It is. It is. It is,' she said.

She was sitting in the hallway on an old wooden stool which creaked with every movement she made. She had her back against the wall to try to keep still but it just made things worse. She swung her feet down and walked towards the front door. It was open. She propped herself against the frame.

'Tell me,' her mother asked. 'Have you been interviewed by the media? You must have been approached?'

She wanted her to put him on the line, so she could talk to him herself.

'He's at the base,' she told her mother, as she watched him pacing the garden looking like a man in love.

'Later, then,' her mother said. 'We'll be up.'

'There is something I have to tell you,' he had said, one day over coffee. This time they had met in Manhattan. They had been involved for two years. Two years of transatlantic crossings. New York was like meeting halfway, but it was clear now that something had to give.

He was nervous, which was unusual, and made her wonder what he was about to say. And then he had told her that he was very probably going to space, which was not what she had expected at all.

'So I'll move to the States,' she had said, resolutely. 'And then you'll move to space.'

They had spent the rest of the day at their hotel. She remembers the cool of the window-pane on her neck as they leant together up above the city.

'I don't know what to do,' she said.

'About what?'

'About you,' she said. He opened his eyes. He was flat out, lengthways, on the sofa. 'About your sleep.'

'It's fine,' he said.

'Is it normal?'

'Early days,' he said.

'Should we check?'

'Early days,' he said again. 'Forget about it.'

'Shouldn't you at least try to regulate? You're becoming nocturnal.' She was surprised at the tone of her voice.

He closed his eyes. 'Yeah. Don't feed me after midnight.'

'Your mother-in-law wants to talk,' she said, walking away.

*

She was awake anyway, but she heard the door, feet on the porch, the squeal of the first step. Switching on the bedside light, she waited. She imagined his slow walk.

When he didn't show, she slipped on shoes and went out, walked the circumference of the house. She checked inside. Maybe she'd been mistaken, maybe he'd been coming in.

She walked to the end of the drive to check the car, and then stood on the verge, looking up and down the road.

She ran through the check-list in her head. She wondered whether she should call the base but knew he would be irritated. Only his sleep, she told herself, had really been affected. He hadn't been gone long. He couldn't have gone far.

She thought about taking the car, driving around the neighbourhood. She pictured herself behind the wheel, trawling the roads, calling his name. It seemed melodramatic.

Because she couldn't imagine going back to sleep she waited, wrapped in the duvet on the porch. She forced herself to think about other things – her article, the man in Sedona she wanted to interview. She sketched a list of questions in her head.

She had always liked the idea of doing interviews but somehow had avoided them so far. She wondered whether she had the necessary pep to be convincing. She couldn't help comparing her relative reserve with the sunny side up, all-American smiles of the women she had come to know.

'Hello, I'm Eleanor Francis,' she said, with vim, extending her hand. 'How are you?' She tried to give the words an energetic spin so they volleyed off the tongue, suggesting untold resources in positive thinking and general can-do. She grinned at the imaginary figure whose fingers were clasped in her own. Her face began to hurt.

'You're up early,' he said. He was on the grass, looking up at her. The first rays of sunlight were edging across the lawn, licking at his bare feet.

'Right,' she said. She felt stoned with lack of sleep.

'I went for a walk.' He shifted his feet in and out of the light. 'I thought I should get some exercise.'

'Right,' she said.

'Gotta take a shower. My feet are really hot.'

He went inside.

*

She watched the sun rise in the corner of their room, stared hard at its white light.

'I'm going away for a few days,' she said, when he came out of the bathroom. 'I have to interview some guy for my work. Okay?'

'A-OK,' he said, rolling into bed with his smile.

She enjoyed driving. She enjoyed waking each day in a new place, grabbing whatever breakfast they offered and then heading out on to the road.

The interstates were long and straight and pretty clear for good stretches. You could really put your foot down. Roads in England were never like this.

At first, changes in the landscape were minor. She passed a sprawling procession of strip towns, with strip malls, and the usual run of roadside food stops: Wendy's, Taco Bell, McDonald's.

Later, when Route 40 took her back to New Mexico and through Albuquerque where they'd first lived, the land seemed to stretch and the sky seemed wide open.

'The shell, as you'll know,' he said, 'is tyres and earth packed together, plastered with adobe.'

He must have been in his sixties. He had shoulder-length white hair, tied back, and had about him a vitality that she found attractive. His skin was weathered – a lifetime spent outdoors.

They walked around the outside of the building together.

'The walls create the thermal mass,' he said. 'The heating and cooling system is completely independent. Inside it's warm in winter, cool in summer.'

They stopped and looked in at a long corridor of plants.

'The greenhouse hallway. South-facing. Waste water gets recycled in the planter.'

'You use pumice, right?'

'And the plants help oxygenate the water. We have vegetables, and some more exotic things.' She could see orchids, banana trees, palm fronds.

Inside was a miracle of sculpted walls and arches, intricate mosaics, rich foliage and water. If you hadn't seen it, you'd find it hard to believe: a sanctuary in this desert of sun-baked red earth.

She walked out a distance from the house with no purpose except to stand in the middle of that expanse; in that heat, on the dry earth. She looked back towards the building. It was like a pale, smooth pebble – like something you could hold in the palm of your hand.

On the terrace, in the evening, she sat with her back warm against the wall, her legs outstretched towards a rusty, shimmering horizon.

'The colour,' she said. 'What is that?'

'Red sandstone, iron oxide, quartz.'

They watched the light fade, the sky deepen. 'Out here,' he said, 'the night is a remarkable thing. You just watch.'

The temperature dropped. The darkness was infinite, spacious.

She woke early – was awake the way she hadn't been since she was a child. She sat in bed, upright, listening to the pre-dawn quiet. She kept her eyes open to the dark, conscious of the warmth of the sheets under the soles of her feet, the cool air on her neck.

She wondered if her husband was awake too. She imagined him listening to the creaking of their timber-frame home. She tried to imagine what he saw as his eyes adjusted, the shapes that presented themselves.

He was one of those people you see every day and start to believe you know when in fact you don't. You have the arrogance to believe they're part of the fabric of your day because you exchange a glance or a smile. You feel they have somehow become part of your life when in fact you have almost nothing to do with them and know nothing about them and haven't made any particular effort with them at all.

He had close-cropped hair. He had black eyes. There was a kind of fluidity to them. They were bright, alert, mobile eyes.

He swept our floor each day. Before the company rehearsed he swept the floor meticulously – I might even say with love. It had become part of the ritual of our day to thoroughly clean the working space. It was part of our company ethic and of the notion we had of discipline. We believed that discipline must matter in the kind of theatre we were hoping to create. We didn't think you could just rock up to rehearsal. Preparing the space was as important as the rehearsal itself.

He swept our floor. He swept it with such love that we stopped sweeping. Before, the task had always been shared. It was part of our ethic that it should be shared. Each actor would be pleased to sweep because each actor knew that sweeping was part of the process of approaching any piece of theatre; the preparation of the space and the readiness for work.

It was because he loved to sweep that we stopped sweeping. It seemed impossibly rude to insist on our right to sweep when he was doing it with so much love. And I'm not being ironic.

I am trying to remember how he came to us. I think he came with the space. We rented the rehearsal room, of course. It was in the very centre of the city, near Berwick Street market where they sell the bread with herbs and olives and those scoops of avocados and plums and whatever's left over at the end of the day for a pound. It was a beautiful space. High up with the rooftops. It must have been a warehouse conversion. It was a broad expanse to work in as an actor. There was enough room to really hurl yourself about. It was so broad that you could create whatever stage space you needed. And up above you it was all skylights – this incredible glass-panelled roof. Like a huge greenhouse. And because you could almost be overwhelmed by the light up there – I mean, if it was sunny it could be intensely bright and hot – there were these expanses of creamy cheesecloth suspended beneath the glass to filter the light. And this cloth would billow like sails – it was like being on a tall ship or something – it was quite wonderful when the breeze came through from the skylights and filled the cloth out. The light would filter through and make the whole place glow, with just the odd shaft of bright light cutting through a gap somewhere and hitting the floor. We were very lucky with this space.

But yes, I think we assumed he must have come with the room. And I remember the morning when the handover, if you like, happened – when it became clear that we would no longer be sweeping for ourselves.

We had all just arrived and were stretching and talking and making coffee and loafing around and Paul I think went to the cupboard in the green room and pulled out the wide broom. They're not strictly brooms, but I don't know another word for them. Sweeper, perhaps. But for spaces like this the wider the better – and they have something like dusters rather than bristles so they run smoothly and don't scratch the surface of the sprung floor. So Paul had taken the sweeper and was just getting started when this man appeared out of nowhere and walked up to him and took it from him and silently started work. And the strange thing was he did it with such authority that – not that Paul would really have fought for the broom – but that, well, none of us dared question him. He belonged to the rehearsal room, quite evidently. And his work was to sweep.

I have to say too that it was almost impossible not to watch him when he swept. It may sound silly or strange or both, but from that first day I found myself drawn to him. I know the others felt the same. I'm sorry to repeat myself but I've told you that he swept with love and I think that had something to do with it. He was intent. He was rapt. He was so completely focused that watching him was like watching theatre. I am trying to explain to you just how impressive he was. It's important for it to make sense – for you to understand how valued he was – because of what happened later.

Though we watched him, he didn't watch us work. He swept in long slow lines across the floor and when he had covered the whole space he left the rehearsal room until the next day. There was no discussion about it. We simply accepted that this was to be the arrangement from the first.

We named him Joe. I realise how it sounds but we never actually found out his name and it got past the point where it would have made any sense to ask. That's why we called him Joe. Not to his face. But we couldn't keep calling him 'the man', or 'the sweep'. We could have made enquiries I suppose. We could have contacted the landlord but it didn't seem necessary – there was no problem. Joe made no demands. He just showed up.

What was strange perhaps was that he always swept in front of us. He didn't do it before we arrived. It didn't matter to us at the time. But for one of us to sweep in front of the others was slightly different because we took it in turns and worked together as a company all day.

You know those horrible plastic chairs you get in assembly rooms and rehearsal rooms and classrooms all over the country? You know the ones that bend in the back where you would hope to have some support from your chair? Well I have the memory of being curled up in one of those chairs inasmuch as you can curl up in one of those chairs: curled, with coffee, script in hand, watching Joe. And the light was coming through the square-paned side-windows and shafting across the floor and it looked like he was walking across sand. He looked as if he was one of those beachcombers with a bleeping treasure-hunter that picks up signals from lost wonders. It looked like he was walking on golden water. He was completely agile and fluid in his movements as he pulled this great sweeper behind him back and forth across the room. I had a completely dead leg when I came to and realised I'd been staring.

I have said we didn't really speak with Joe. Well, I always said 'Hey' to him, I'm sure, or gave him a smile or a glance that said 'Hey'. But our dynamic wasn't about chat. And I know it was clear to him how much I admired the way he worked. You don't stare at someone the way I did without good reason.

I soon found that I couldn't imagine rehearsing without first seeing Joe. It sounds ridiculous, but I couldn't think how we'd managed before. Our working day now had about it that sense of ritual we had aimed for but never properly achieved. Somehow, with Joe's presence each morning, our work seemed more significant. We approached rehearsals with a greater sense of pride and sobriety. We didn't arse around as much as we used to. We were more focused. We got more done.

I realised I associated Joe with that room, and with the feeling I had there of space and of the ability to work so willingly and well. The light, that lofty ceiling and Joe's fluid movement and strong focus and bright eyes – all of these bound together in my mind. I couldn't imagine him existing anywhere else. And I loved that space. I couldn't imagine working anywhere else. I felt so blessed to be there with the cries of birds and the sounds drifting up from the market and the small, cool breeze that came into the room with that liquid light.

Then one day Joe was late. There had never been any trouble with timing. But this one day he was late. And I felt – we all felt – that we should wait for him. Maybe it was crazy, but it just didn't seem right to start without him. It would've felt like a jinx. So we were holding on waiting for Joe and feeling strangely compelled to wait. We didn't even run lines. We hung around and did nothing. We were actively waiting for Joe so that we could begin.

So we waited, and he was an hour late. The fact is we should have got on with the rehearsal or bloody well swept for ourselves but we didn't and so wasted precious time. And then he arrived and made no apology and went straight for the broom to start sweeping. And as he did, John said loudly in this ridiculously stupid Queen's English voice, 'Buck up, old chap!'

Joe took the broom from the cupboard, as always. He held it aloft with one steady arm as he made his way out of the green room, stepping over the feet and bags and cups of coffee that cluttered the floor. With his other arm he pushed open one half of the swing doors that led into the rehearsal room and as soon as he was through he pulled the two long arms of the sweeper into line, lowered them until they were suspended about an inch above the surface of the floor, and after the briefest of pauses let them drop and started work. Nothing in his actions would have given away that he was hurt.

But from that day I saw a change. There was an awareness that he was sweeping in front of us. He was self-conscious somehow, as if he didn't want to be watched, as if we weren't welcome any more. He was as thorough as ever, but his sweeping seemed pointed in a way it hadn't before. I guess I was hurt. It didn't seem to me now that he swept with love, and I got less and less pleasure from watching him work.

It just happened that at this point the company started working longer hours. We were coming up to a preview performance, and the pressure was on a little more than usual. It is at these times that routine matters more than ever as it works against the inevitable jitters. It is however also at these times that it is most tempting to let routine go to hell and cut out any preamble to rehearsal that doesn't seem essential. As certain as we felt that sweeping was a crucial part of our rehearsal ritual, it was always one of the first things to go when we were under pressure.

It wouldn't have been a big issue one way or the other if we'd been the ones doing it. We simply would've stopped. However, it wasn't us doing it, and because John had been rude we felt stuck. We simply couldn't find it in ourselves to tell Joe to stop.

So instead, worse than that, we gradually, inevitably, morning by morning, made it clear how inconvenient it was. You can perhaps imagine the scenario. Those annoying little things that people have it in them to do: a cough here, a glance at a watch there or, with actors, a session of ostentatious stretching beside the rehearsal room floor. Not a word spoken but a prevalent, malevolent sense of focus on this one person who has become an obstacle. None of it made him stop. He continued his routine as if we were not there. Instead, strangely, we felt more and more self-conscious. We felt we were being watched. We felt sure that his black eyes were fixed on us from somewhere beyond the swing doors as we rehearsed.

Our desire to put an end to the sweeping soon developed into a complex. In our conversations we confirmed with each other that Joe was freaking us out. Not only that, but he had taken what was ours away from us. It was for us to do. He had no right. It was part of our process. He wasn't an actor. We could see that it was of the utmost importance that we should reclaim this activity which had been stolen from us, leaving us impotent and quarrelsome just days before our preview. Did he not have the sensitivity to realise that he should just leave?

It had reached the point of the ridiculous. We drew straws one evening over drinks and it fell upon John to speak to Joe a second time.

'No. I'm sorry. This has gone on long enough,' is what he said, sternly, the next morning in the green room. 'You're not welcome here. Can't you see you're not wanted? You're going to have to leave.' I think that is pretty much what he said. We were all gathered for the big moment, clutching our coffees and bottles of water for reassurance.

But Joe, impassive, broom in hand, crossed the room, and said only, 'No. That won't be possible.' That's all he said.

I don't think any of us could believe it. John for once looked lost for words and just stood there watching as Joe made his way yet again through the swing doors to the rehearsal room. I looked at John and the others and it was obvious that no one was going to say or do anything and I was so furious I could feel this buzzing in my head and I followed Joe through the swing doors and walked right in front of him so that he would have to stop sweeping and look at me. I was so angry I could feel my heart pumping and my cheeks flushing and then there he was, just looking at me steadily with those bright, black eyes, saying nothing, so I took a step towards him and brought up my hand and I slapped him hard across the cheek. I could see the colour changing on his cheek but it wasn't changing fast enough so I slapped him again.

I'd hit this man whose name I didn't know because he wouldn't stop sweeping for us for free. It was impossible then to stay – in that space up with the rooftops and the light and the window drapes that billowed like sails. And so I left.

On the far side the lake is divided from the hills by a slash of soft pink that arrived with the dawn.

They set out, stepping over a yawning crack where the ice has buckled. All along the shoreline the lake has twisted, churning the ice into contortions which it has thrown up and aside, forming banks of frozen rubble softened only by fresh snowfall. Ahead of them the ice smooths out, leaving its fretted edges behind, coursing towards the other side.

They would normally carry their father's bore, or fishing rods, or both, but their hands are empty. Having made their decision they wrapped themselves up with every layer they could find. Yet still they are lung-punched, speechless for now with the cold.

It is so early that the last of the stars are still out. The morning is clear. Pyotr imagines them seen from the hillside up above the village behind – two dark figures against all that white. He had once climbed up there with his father and they had looked out from maybe a thousand metres up, and he had seen the tiny, matchbox houses below and the people, splinter-small. The lake had looked narrow – like a river, like something you could just step across.

He stops and looks back.

He sees the row of wooden houses, the roofs and windows with their splashes of blue paint, their own a straightforward brown. He sees the red iron girders of the railway. He sees the thin line of smoke rising from behind their home where they had left their father standing at the brazier. He would not be watching them.

A little way along the shoreline a turquoise boat sits, prow facing the frozen waters, its colour sprung alive against the snow.

Turning, he sees his brother some way ahead of him now, a small figure with a red balaclava moving out across the ice. To the north, which they'll keep on their right-hand side as they walk, the lake stretches off, far away beyond, four hundred miles.

When they reach the fishing huts – miniature shelters thrown together from wood and tarpaulin a few hundred feet from the shore – they stop. It is automatic. This is as far as either of them has been on the ice before. In the summer, with their father, they had gone out in the boat much further than this, but never on the ice.

'People drive cars over all of the time,' Pyotr says.

'I know.' Golom plants himself on a wooden crate beside one of the huts. He curls his mittens into imperfect binoculars and surveys the scene from his perch. 'I'm not scared,' he says. 'Are you?'

Pyotr throws him a scornful look. 'It's March.' The ice would be solid for at least another month. It wasn't until late April – May, even – that it started to melt and pull apart. 'Come on,' he says, swivelling his feet around.

They walk in silence keeping up a good pace. Pyotr's eyes are on the thin band of colour that seems to be hovering above the far shore.

His earliest memories are of his father heading off on to the ice, and returning hours later, breath steaming, the skin on his face burning with the cold and the exertion. As a child, he would marvel at the chapped skin of his hands, their leathery feel. He remembers him coming in from a snowstorm, clapping both large palms around his own soft hands, and the shock of cold-heat that transferred itself from his father's skin to his own. He remembers watching over and over, from the yard or from the window, as his father disappeared into that limitless expanse; slowly moving, slowly shrinking. His mother, in these memories, is no more than an awareness – the sense of her like a pulse that travels up his spine, keeping his back straight, his eyes sharp. She must have been there then, those times, close by, maybe even at his side, but he finds it hard now to remember her face. It is seven years since she died. They have only one photograph, and in it she doesn't look like herself.

'What have we got to eat?' Golom asks. His cheeks are flushed with the cold and his eyes are streaming, but he has the sleepy stare of still waking up. His breath comes in clouds.

'You'd know if you'd packed the bag,' Pyotr says. 'You'd know if you were the one carrying it.'

'I'm smaller than you.'

'You're stubbier.'

Before being re-christened Golom he was known as Stubby on account of his stockiness and strength. Although he was only small, he had impressed even their father with a natural toughness, an ability to endure physical strains with a degree of joy. He seemed still to surprise himself with this facility, as if he'd just woken up to discover secret powers.

'I can carry the bag too, can't I?' he asks.

'Yes you can,' says Pyotr. 'We'll change over halfway.'

'How will we know when we're halfway?'

'It'll be obvious.' Pyotr waits for his brother to challenge him on this but he doesn't. You never could tell when he would suddenly decide he'd had enough and want the answers to everything.

Last summer a man had come to the lake to do experiments. He was part of an environmental team, and came to their father's yard wanting use of a boat. He spoke Russian – which was why he had been sent ahead of his group to set things up. He knew everything about the lake and what was in it. He was the one who had given Stubby his new name.

Stubby was incredible in the water; not only could he stay in far longer than anyone else without feeling the cold, but somehow he just couldn't float on the surface, and had learnt to let himself sink to the bottom and dwell down there like a fish, only now and then coming up for air. The man – Dec-Lan – had never seen anything like it. He had wanted to research Stubby's condition and find out the proper name for it. The boys had not known before then that it was the sort of thing to have its own name.

Dec-Lan had rechristened Stubby after the small fish that existed only in this lake; the golomyanka. Dec-Lan told Stubby that most people who swam for long times in cold water had to rub fat all over their skin. The golomyanka was over 35% fat and lived deep down in the water. Dec-Lan told Stubby he was more golomyanka than boy.

'It's like you have a wetsuit under your skin,' he said. 'We'll have to take you to the lab and have a closer look.'

Stubby had looked wary until Dec-Lan's face cracked into a smile.

'*You're-all-right*,' Dec-Lan had said, in English. This was something he said a good bit, '*You're-all-right*.' Pyotr couldn't be sure what it meant, but he liked the sound, the way the words came out.

Far ahead of them he can see conifers, and birches – slivers of upright silver, lining the banks of the lake. With their father they have been to the forests where the trees are lined up like ghostly battalions, clouding the horizon in layered multitudes, even then barely there. Dead souls, their mother would have said.

Her curiosity towards old superstitions had come laced with a love of ambiguity. Details so familiar they were considered fact would be entirely altered. She would decide for herself, as the mood took her, who was good and who was evil among the lake spirits. You could never tell how a story would end. Pyotr never could decide whether the lake island was home to a demon and, as many times as they had made the trip out there in his father's boat, he had yet to set foot on shore.

The sun is making its slow ascent. The air is empty, noiseless. The sound of their feet alone.

Pyotr stops, closes his eyes.

'What?' Golom asks.

'Stop.'

'What is it?'

'Stop talking.'

'What?'

'Just shut up.'

He hears his brother step closer to him and then stop. They stand beside each other listening. For a moment, there is no sound at all.

'I can't hear anything,' Golom says.

'Exactly.'

'*Jay-sus.*' This was something else Dec-Lan had said.

Smiling, Pyotr opens his eyes and sees snow falling like lazy butterflies. Golom starts leaping, waving his arms around him and clapping his hands together to try to catch the flakes. Pyotr feels the cold drops of moisture landing on his face. 'Stop jumping around,' he says to Golom. 'You'll use all your energy.' Golom stands still and tries instead to catch a snowflake on his tongue. 'Do that too long, your tongue will freeze and drop off.' Golom looks circumspect; he starts flicking his tongue in and out rapidly, like a lizard, or a frog. A moment later he stops.

'When can we eat?'

'When do you want to eat?'

'Now.' He looks defiant. He knows it's too early.

They eat watching the snow fall around them. It seems to be coming out of nowhere. There are wisps of cloud up above, nothing more.

Golom sits with the backpack flat beneath him, his legs stretched out in front. He looks towards home, then to the far bank, and then back again towards home. 'How far have we come?' he asks. He takes another bite of bread. He sits there chewing, swinging his legs open and shut like windscreen wipers on the ice.

Pyotr tries to gauge the distance. 'A few miles,' he says.

'How many exactly?'

'Maybe five?'

'Five?'

'Maybe.'

Golom has stopped moving his legs and is sitting very still now, peering through the ice.

'Anything down there?' Pyotr asks. He remembers when they went out on the water, and Dec-Lan told tales about pre-historic crocodiles lurking just beneath the boat and Golom shivered with delight.

'All we ever have is smoked fish,' Golom says.

Beneath them the ice is glistening silver in the early light. Pyotr always felt that you should be able to see right through to the water beneath. Sometimes it looked so transparent – it

seemed to him there should be something down there waiting to be seen.

He remembers sitting in the boat with his father as somewhere
beneath them Dec-Lan swam. He didn't really understand
what he got up to down there. He imagined him sometimes swimming, sometimes floating, looking about, bubbles
streaming from his mask. When he reappeared Pyotr found
it hard not to look pleased. Dec-Lan would be grinning as he
flung his arms over the side and pulled himself up, landing
black and shiny in his wetsuit at their feet. '*Jay-sus!*'

His father didn't speak to Dec-Lan. He would guide the
boat out on to the lake until he was asked to stop, and then
cut the engine. If they began to drift he would use the oars
to adjust their position.

Golom lies flat on his back now. 'How much longer will it
take?' he says.

'Are you tired?'

'No.'

'Are you sure?'

'Yes.'

'Maybe an hour,' Pyotr says. 'Maybe it'll take an hour.'

His brother starts making duck noises, staring at the sky.
He pulls an invisible rifle from his shoulder, aims, fires.

'Have you finished eating?'

'Yes.'

'Do you want some tea?'

'No.'

'Let's go.'

Pyotr watches Golom slowly getting to his feet and regrets having stopped so early. He feels somehow they have lost momentum, that they should have kept going and eaten as they went.

At the far side the ice is gleaming coolly in the sunlight.

As they set off again he tries to get a sense of the distances involved. He looks towards the southern end of the lake. A landmark would make things easier, but there are only the usual scatterings of houses lining the banks. He needs something like the paper mill that will mark out their home from the other side, when they look back.

He wonders whether he should have brought a map, or a compass, though the thought had not crossed his mind when he packed his bag. He had never seen his father use these things. It was a clear day, conditions were perfect. When people talked about the breadth of the lake they talked about the farthest reaches, where it was forty miles across, not here, where it tapered. The distance was nothing in comparison. When he found out, his father probably wouldn't even be impressed.

Pyotr had spent his childhood familiar with the smells of the boatyard. His father brought home the tar and the varnish, though he would wash in the shower he had rigged outside their home before coming in to eat.

Sometimes Pyotr would lean out of a window to watch as his father snarled under the cold water. 'Over here!' he would yell, and his father would play-act some forest creature, straining his arms towards him, gnashing his teeth. When he reappeared, freshly washed, traces of the yard would still betray him – spots and stains on the skin of his face and forearms.

One morning late last summer, he had caught Pyotr by the sleeve, brought him to the yard, and planted him on the smooth, warm hull of an overturned boat. 'Watch,' was all he had said. Pyotr had tried to watch, though he couldn't see the point, not knowing what it was that he was watching. Men moved around the yard, stopping occasionally to exchange a word, wandering inexplicably in and out of the large shed that housed the equipment. No one paid him any attention. He appeared to have been forgotten.

He sat there in the heat and his eyelids became weighted. Soon enough he watched the yard through the thicket of his lashes. He tried to keep his eyes focused on his father's figure, but it elongated, distorted. He felt his head slump once, twice.

He woke to the sound of laughter. He was on the ground at the foot of the hull, crumple-curled like a baby, drool trailing from one side of his mouth. His father and the others working the yard were standing over him – one of the men crying with mirth, his face creased up.

His father had stepped forward and pulled him to his feet. 'You'd better stick with me,' he said.

The boats that he took on did not belong to rich men, but to working men like himself. The way he worked was instinctive. He approached each craft with respect. He had an understanding and a love of the jigsaw of pieces that made them up, the texture and history of the wood. 'What can we do to get you shipshape?' he would ask under his breath as he paced around a boat, assessing it for himself, regardless of what he had been told. He didn't waste time when he got to work.

Pyotr stood all day watching his father. At dusk they walked home. He fell into bed, turned his face to the wall, slept.

When he was asked the next day if he would be coming to the yard he surprised himself by saying yes. By the end of the week he was pleased with the welts and scars that were collecting on his skin. His hands had blistered. His arms had developed muscles he had not known existed as he stripped and varnished the boats.

'What are we going to do when we reach the other side?' Golom asks. He is keeping up, but stops every few paces to take one step back before carrying on.

'Do you have to do that?'

'What?' Golom asks, this time taking two steps back.

'What makes you think we'll reach the other side?' Pyotr says. 'I'll have dealt with you long before then.'

Jay-sus!' Golom darts ahead. 'You'll have to catch me.' He stops briefly, waits until Pyotr has nearly caught up with him, and then shoots off again. He is laughing a wheezy kind of laugh. He thinks he's funny. He keeps it going a good while – picking up speed by skidding in short bursts.

Pyotr has no plan for the other side except to catch a lift. If they are lucky with their timing they can try to hitch the school bus that runs the western stretch. That would take them a good way. They would be in before dark.

He is warm inside his cocoon of clothes. His legs are getting used to the rhythm. He pictures the schoolroom – Limpet, chalk in hand; his classmates casting wondering glances towards his empty chair. He breathes in deeply and puffs out white flurries, imagining that it is smoke from a cigar, or cigarette.

He didn't think Limpet would bother to call his father.

There is a fissure an inch, two inches wide, tracing a path across the ice ahead of them. They stand looking down at it.

'It's nothing,' Pyotr says. 'It's just a crack.'

They take a step closer.

'There's no melt water,' he says.

Golom squats on the ice and lowers his hand into the crevice, pulls it out quickly, and lowers it again. He looks up at Pyotr, squinting in the sunlight, and releases a chuckle, something like a growl, from deep down in his throat.

'Come on,' Pyotr says.

The sun is much higher in the sky now.

They follow the same path as the crevice, pausing to inspect it now and then where it widens, and then carrying on. It meanders a little, but not much. It seems to be heading the way they want to go. They walk side by side, either side of it, keeping the far reaches of the lake on their right.

The way the crevice is etched in the ice reminds him of the fracture that still runs the length of their bedroom wall.

He remembers waking from his sleep to what he believed was a train going past, heavy with freight. His bed was vibrating. He had reached out and put one hand against the wall and found that it was pulsing too. And then he had heard the urgency in his father's voice. They had stood in the doorway. The next day they saw the fracture in the wall, and downstairs, plaster littering the floor like dirty snowfall.

Dec-Lan knew about fault lines, and tectonic plates, and volcanoes.

He was a geologist, with a sideline in marine biology – that was what he had said. He had swum deep down in the ocean near Iceland, and waited, and listened, and heard the sound of the earth pulling itself apart.

In the autumn, on the map on the school wall, Pyotr had found Iceland. He had put his finger on top of it, pressed down hard. He remembers Dec-Lan walking along the shore with the wetsuit pulled to his waist. He remembers the plastic shoes that he wore in the water, and that squelched when he walked.

'I am a geologist, with a sideline in marine biology,' Pyotr says, under his breath, as he walks. Dec-Lan had said that one day their lake would become an ocean, with the movement of the plates, the shifting of the earth.

'If we're going to do this hike across your lake,' he had said with a wink, 'we'd better do it soon.'

Pyotr stops and takes in the ice all around them, the distance they have to go until they reach the shore.

He imagines the vibration building, travelling through his body, making its way from his feet, through his calves, up his legs.

It would be slow at first – tiny fractures in the ice, barely visible, pencil marks scored across the lake. The sound would be glass shattering; a million splinters.

A sudden force and his vision blurs – his head thrown side to side, backwards and forwards. He sucks in great raw breaths of air. He is staggering, reeling, feet spreadeagled. When the ice ruptures, the noise is deafening. It is the sound of cities collapsing. The lake breaks into craggy, bobbing chunks. There is a final, fatal, immersion in the water.

Pyotr finds the lake still solid beneath their feet; but the air is changing. It becomes filmy, taking new form, cascading in gossamer curtains that filter the sunlight, sending it shafting in every direction at once. The sky vanishes. They are drenched in light and water – suspended with no above and no below. And then the mist thickens to a white-out. Pyotr can't see his hands as he holds them to his face and when he looks down his feet have gone.

'Where are you?' he says.

No response.

'Hey. Where are you?'

'I'm right here. *Jay-sus*,' Golom says, close by.

'Well, don't wander off. Stay put.'

They stand there in silence for a moment. It is incredibly quiet. Pyotr can feel a fine cold spray falling on his skin. He hears Golom sigh and wonders how long it is going to last. His eyes are open, looking up and around to see what he can see, but there is nothing.

'I can see a face,' Golom says.

'No you can't.'

'I can see a face.'

'Don't be stupid.' He tries not to think about the lake spirits.

He tries not to think about the fissure.

Golom starts humming tunelessly, loudly. Pyotr knows that he's doing it to be annoying and is about to tell him to shut up, but finds that he likes it. He doesn't say a word. He stands in the middle of the white-out, smiling.

Dec-Lan's smiles would come and go easily and he was not used to this, did not know how to respond. Instead of just smiling back he would find himself staring. Dec-Lan would laugh – not unkindly – but he would laugh at him.

The mist lifts abruptly and space opens out just as quickly as it had disappeared.

The sun is bright in the sky. The air feels fresh. They walk on.

Later in the summer Dec-Lan's team arrived with its own boat, and Pyotr would see them heading out much further than they had been in his father's small craft. There they would use sonar, and specialist diving equipment, and they would do tests underwater. He was told this at school, when the whole class was told about it in the autumn – the group of scientists who had come to study their lake, and who were now long gone.

Pyotr had watched the boat head out early in the morning

from the other side, where they had set up their base. It followed the same route each time up the far shore. He had imagined Dec-Lan standing on the deck of the boat looking out. Pyotr would wave. He couldn't see anyone waving back, but doing it made him still feel connected to the man.

Dec-Lan had told them their lake was fifty million years old, four hundred miles long. He had told them that many of the species in the lake could only be found in this one lake in the whole world. He had told them that the geology of the area – the volcanoes, the earthquakes – was phenomenal. He had told them that the weather systems blew his mind – those storms, he said, that came in out of nowhere; those hurricanes; those monumental waves. 'I want to see that for myself,' he had said. 'I have to see that.'

At their feet the fissure has widened into something more impressive: a hole. It isn't a fishing hole. It's natural. The sides are smooth – polished even – vivid in the light. It is whorled like a shell, and changes colour gradually from white to sky-blue as it descends. It darkens finally into something deeper – like someone poured ink down there.

They lie, flat on their bellies, looking in. It's like peering down a well. They can hear water at the bottom – gurgling and sloshing about.

'Haalllooo!' Pyotr calls.

'Haalllooo!' It calls back.

'Ooooolla!' Golom yells.

'Ooooolla!' It yells back.

Golom rolls over, victorious, and lets out a cry. It takes flight.

Pyotr pulls the flask and the remainders of their lunch from the backpack. They eat, cross-legged, smiling like guardians at the mouth of the hole, before moving on.

'When we get to the other side,' Pyotr says, 'I reckon we can catch the bus.'

He thinks they're making good time. They are moving faster now, eager for the other side. The air feels charged, somehow alive.

'Imagine their faces,' Golom says.

Pyotr glances at his brother. 'I reckon we should play it down.'

Golom doesn't look convinced.

'If we get back early enough, we could just not tell,' Pyotr says.

'Dad?'

'Right.'

'Why?'

'So someone else would. It'd be better that way. He'd be really impressed because we hadn't even mentioned it ourselves.'

Golom's mouth falls open. He looks stunned. 'I'm telling him,' he says.

'That's fine.'

'I'm telling him.'

'If that's what you want.'

'I am.'

'That's OK,' Pyotr says. 'You're too young to understand.'

Golom hits him side on, knocking him back down on to the ice. He's all fists and rage. Though Pyotr tries to push him off he can't and soon he gives up and just takes the pelting.

'Take it back!' Golom shrieks, high-pitched.

'No.'

'Take it back!'

'Why would I take it back?' He's laughing but the fist-fall is starting to hurt. 'OK. Stop it.' He tries once more to shake Golom off.

'Take it back!'

'OK. I take it back. I take it back.'

They lie flat out on the ice catching their breath. Though the sun is still bright the blue has faded.

Pyotr cranes his head and looks at things upside down. He sees the paper mill, inverted, the building like a large pale bug, its legs in the air, the stilt-like props reaching up towards the earth.

'Train!' Golom yells.

All their lives they had heard the sound of it, and if they were quick enough caught sight of it too, steam streaming behind, faces pressed to the windows. It went to Vladivostok, to the ocean. They had to imagine what that was like – water to the other side of the world.

'We should probably get up,' Pyotr says, making no attempt to move. He looks along the shoreline for their home. He sees brittle trees lined up like ghost people, mountains behind.

Dec-Lan had arrived on the train. He had come with his talk of lichen and gastropods and crustaceans. He had told them he never wanted to go, never wanted to leave these shores, these forests, these mountains.

The colour of the shore has changed – a deep, bruised blue underscores the mountainside ahead. Pyotr looks at his brother. 'Let's go,' he says. 'Not far now.' He gets to his feet and pulls up his scarf. Golom fixes his balaclava so it covers his nose, but then yanks it back down. He is smiling. 'I can carry the bag now,' he says. 'You said.' As soon as he has the backpack they get going. The disc of the sun is now faint in the sky, glowing white on white behind gathering clouds.

Pyotr has known moments when the air and the land have taken on the look of an old photograph – everything washed with a kind of gold-brown, every detail picked out. This is happening now. Every tree trunk, every leafless branch, every roof, the sliver of the road running parallel to the shore – which is close now – the layered foothills, the mountains behind. Everything is carefully drawn.

'Look,' he says.

'What?'

'Do you see that?' he says. He pulls down his scarf, stops to take it all in. He turns very slowly on the spot. 'You see that?' he shouts out, punching at the air with his fist.

Golom is pointing to the shore ahead of them. The ice has turned a muddy kind of black where it meets the beach.

Hail – suddenly – stinging the skin. It comes in horizontally.

'Cover up,' Pyotr says. 'Shit.'

Golom is looking at him and his mouth is open but no words are coming out, or if there are words they are being taken by the wind which is starting to howl at them like something malevolent come to life. Icy water is streaming down his face.

'Cover up,' Pyotr calls into the wind. 'Cover your face!'

His brother is immobile. His eyes are wide and scared.

'Hold on to me,' Pyotr shouts into his ear. 'Hold on. OK?' He tries to tug the balaclava over his brother's face as he pulls him in.

The wind whips at them, buffeting. And snow now. A blinding white mass.

Pyotr's legs are knocked sideways as the full force hits them, his feet threatening to slip from under him. Keep steady, he tells himself. Hold on.

As close as he is to his brother he can no longer make out the features of his face. 'Stubby?' he yells. But it is pointless. There is no way of speaking or hearing in this. The wind cuts through to his skin, which is prickling, startled. His fingers are burning.

Closing his eyes against the squall he thinks how if he'd asked his father before heading off he would have known the answers to any question of distance, or orientation, or the time it would take them to cross the lake if they walked at a particular speed.

He pictures his father. And then he tries to picture his mother too. She's strange and serious. Like the photograph. He tries to remember her voice instead – the warmth of it – but what he hears is the wind.

The sound that makes it through his layers reminds him of the time he had water trapped in his ears after swimming, the feeling of being still submerged, the true sound of the world gone, speech lost, his own voice distorted even to himself, the noises inside his body magnified, the sounds outside that were normally so clear changed into something strange and rushing, and creaky and complaining, like a haunted house.

Now he is with Dec-Lan suspended underwater, listening for the sound of the plates. His feet are moving slowly to keep himself in place. His arms are spread wide like an eagle, and he is smiling.

'Wake up,' he tells himself somewhere deep down. 'Swim.'

He cannot feel his arms holding his brother. His lashes are thick with snow now and he blinks to see, to reassure himself that he still has him. He's there – he sees his red balaclava – although he doesn't trust himself, doesn't trust his hands to hold on. He bends his knees and manoeuvres himself down on to the ice, brings Golom with him, covers his body with his own, tries to shield him from the wind and the snow.

Hovering in his mind, delicate, alive: his brother's wide eyes – irises like crystals, white-blue, pale and splintered.

'*You're-all-right,*' he murmurs to him now.

His daughter will not wake up.

Sunlight has taken the blinds. They glow amber. Still her eyes are closed. She is inert; so deep inside herself that even breath seems unlikely.

She has slept, long into the mornings, and later, on through the afternoons, for weeks now. The times she would usually wake up, and get up, he can't help but be drawn to her room to see if today, maybe.

She sleeps. She is the age when she should be out in the world, inquisitive, demanding, and yet she sleeps. She should be calling from elsewhere, calling him at inappropriate times, at times suitable to her but not to him. Visiting, she should be bringing home friends, lovers even.

She should not be home now.

When he has got up, and washed, had coffee and toast, and when he has checked in with work in his study downstairs, he makes his way up the small flight of stairs to her room, and for a few moments then at the start of each day he puts himself on pause, he waits with her: he watches her sleeping.

Her mother comes to visit, sometimes; she has a tough schedule. She finds it upsetting. She has always been easily upset. When she comes she leaves a trail of things for their daughter – flowers, clothes. The first time, she sat on the edge of her bed and said, 'You're young and you're lovely. What is this?'

She wasn't the only one asking.

The day his daughter called and asked to be picked up from college, the afternoon he spent packing up her stuff that only weeks before had been unpacked in her shared room, the evening they arrived home and he unlocked the front door and watched her creeping like an old woman towards her childhood bed, it was certainly on his mind. What is this?

There are things he won't let himself think.

But he is a great believer in change. He believes that it happens whether we like it or not. He believes in the patience game. He believes that somewhere, under the surface, she is working it all out for herself.

She baffled the doctors. They puzzled over her, and then they let her be. She didn't want pills, a counsellor. If this is a great puzzling out for her, he thinks, it is private, and contained, and kept like a secret deep in her body.

People ask him, How is she? He doesn't know what to say. They tell him: You are so accepting. It must be so frustrating. They seem to want something from him; want acknowledgement perhaps that without a name it's insubstantial, unreasonable, this state she is in. They want to crack the surface of her, and let the secret out.

He once had a thorn in his heel. He had felt a small sting with each step he took, but seeing nothing on the surface of the skin ignored it. It took months, but the thing worked its way out, arriving one day in a cloud of infected glory. It was about an inch long – a splinter. It had been lodged deep in his foot all that time, and he walking about.

He thinks of this when he finds himself hurting about the way his daughter is. How she doesn't seem to feel anything. How oblivious she seems. How numb.

When she is cocooned in sleep the passivity of her face seems less strange to him. In sleep, he hopes, everything falls away. It is when she is awake that he finds that expressionless oval troubling. It reminds him of devotional paintings: the downcast gaze and unlined skin of a Madonna.

He is a great believer in life being lived, not held in reserve.

His daughter's hands are not working as they should. When he collected her from the college room he had to tie the laces on her shoes.

If she gets to washing, he fills a sink, and then she can splash her body and her face for herself. If she gets to dressing, she somehow puts on the basics and then accepts his help. When she needs to brush her teeth he has to do that.

He reads to her. He started this about a month in when the appointments had stopped, and the well-wisher visits, and when he realised his hopes for her were, for the moment, futile. He doesn't ask what she would like him to read, because it is when she is sleeping. He reads, and after a while he stops.

At first he had read fairy tales because that was the book beside her bed. He did not know whether it was there by choice – it perhaps simply had always been, since childhood.

He started reading from a how-to manual a couple of months in. As an engineer they made sense to him, those clear instructions on ways to achieve practical results. Here there was definition. Here there was cause and effect. He read to her about putting up shelves, and fixing a washer in a tap, and unblocking a sink.

He could have told her about his work; how buildings are designed to give, how towers are made to sway in strong winds. He could have told her how wind turbines might soon be sent up into the sky to hang like kites, mobile, aloft, at the end of long cords. He could have told her all about the conversion of kinetic energy, how wind becomes electricity.

But instead, when he was finished with the how-to manual, he had started on teaching her how to drive. In a way, he preferred this. He could set up a car in the middle of her room and do the thing he was describing. He could not put up shelves – there was no need, and of course the noise. There was no washer in her room; no tap, no sink. He improvised a car for himself, right there, and for a fortnight spent time running through the drill. 'I should be an instructor, don't you think?' he said to his silent daughter, his hand resting on the nub of his father's walking stick – which, with the help of the umbrella stand, served as an elevated gear shift. He was calm, and patient – though what else could he be? He surprised himself by not feeling idiotic. Most times, with words – his own words – he did. Most times, especially when it mattered, he was embarrassed, and felt he said the wrong thing. When his parents were sick he had found it impossible to find his way there, to words.

There were many things you did not speak of with a daughter. You chose, most of the time, not to invade her privacy. You did not pry. You kept a respectful distance. You left the talking to the women. But when all the talking was done there were times when things were still, and calm: when you could sit down and simply share a moment, and see a thing for what it was – not all chatter.

His daughter had been teenage, but childlike still. And never so far from him as this.

She had told him that back when it started, a friend had raided a local nursing home and brought an old wheelchair to college. She had been embarrassed, but allowed him to carry her down the stairs, and through the foyer, in front of everyone, and then out into the waiting contraption – a rug tucking her in.

Her friend had taken her along the coast. They couldn't go on the beach, not with the wheels, and so had followed the track behind the dunes, where cars beetled along to park, where there were skateboarders and cyclists. Her friend had pushed her along, she said, really fast, so the wheels on the wheelchair were rattling and she thought the whole thing would fall apart. He had run with her as fast as he could, into the wind.

His daughter had told him that she could sense their speed, but even though her body was jumping about, and she could see the chair was vibrating like mad from the rough tarmac beneath the wheels, she could not feel a thing. She was numb.

She told him this. She had watched the dune grass blown about, and the kites, and the clouds. She had watched the waves pouring themselves on to the sand. She had watched her hair blasted by the wind, blown demented. She could see that it was attached to her head, and yet it was a distant thing.

When they are done with cars, he has decided they will move on to aircraft. He will read to her from manuals on how to fly a plane. He will read to her about the rocket engine, and the dynamics of gliding. He will read to her about speed and motion.

BLACKOUT

New York City. A sticky, impossible heat. The hottest July since records began. The sidewalks stink. The rubbish in the apartment stinks. Everywhere, small blasts of air suggest small deaths, heat rot. Down in the subway, slick with sweat, everyone melts.

At the eye clinic Sean signs in. He fills out a form. When he takes it back to the man at the sign-in station he is told to wait; and so he waits with his form on the edge of a room already full of people waiting. Up above them, on a boxy television set, a javelin arcs through the air. The Olympics are on, though no one seems to be watching.

'You'll have to pay.' The receptionist smiles at him vaguely. She waves his passport at a colleague, and through the thick plastic screen dividing patients from staff he hears the muffled echo, 'He'll have to pay.'

He knows he'll have to pay. The only insurance they accept here is local, affiliated. You claim later. You pay up front. He knows.

'I know that,' he says. His voice, he thinks, sounds calm.

'I'll need a certificate,' he says, 'for insurance, for when I get back home.'

He had been eight when he presented with night blindness; he could not see in half-light, could not see the stars on a clear night.

His mother had prepared for the worst, like a doomsday believer stockpiling food, amassing an arsenal of weapons. It was likely a case of recessive genes. She told him she thought she was the carrier. Her father had been blind at forty-one.

The consultant had suggested sunglasses, vitamin A, but Diane pushed her son to be prepared, wanting him to have the confidence to cope on his own. Knowing he might go blind when she was gone, she drilled him, drawing on skills her father used.

She walked her son around their home in a blindfold. She watched as, sightless, with one of her headscarves patterning his face, he learnt to cross his room, to locate himself within the space. She taught him to stick to routine, to place his belongings in a regular spot he could easily find. 'If it happens,' she said, 'wherever you are, this is what you are going to have to do.'

Typed on a small pink sheet above the check-in desk upstairs, *Para los Walk-In*, and beside it: *Healing in Progress! ¡Silencio, por Favor!* In the chill of air conditioning, row upon row of seats. Row upon row of people waiting. They look to have been there a while. Some are blinking, some rubbing at their eyes, some sleeping. Several wear sunglasses despite being inside.

Sean takes a seat facing the double doors to the clinic. They are opaque, designed for privacy, swinging open now and then to eject a processed patient. High up on the wall another antiquated television set, and again, the Olympics: talking heads between events.

The light of the screen bothers him. He looks away.

Close by, a woman sits curled over, a lemon-yellow blanket on her shoulders, her eyes closed tight. On either side of her are girls, likely her daughters, with hoodies up. A lanky guy in cowboy boots has crumpled in his seat; one arm hangs low so the back of his hand rests on the floor. Along from Sean another man – huge and sweaty, his damp hair pasted – swabs his brow.

Sean closes his eyes. He hears flip-flops passing, sucking greedily.

After a time, as a child, he had known his way about at night. He stopped bumping into things. He stopped staring into the darkness as if it might ease, as if he might start to see. He turned brisk and practical, was short with himself if he collided with an object as he traced a path across his room. 'No, you dumbo,' he muttered. He learnt to use his hands with confidence, to reach out and interpret what he felt.

In daylight, blindfolded, he learnt to use a cane. He and Diane walked the garden. They walked an orchard belonging to a neighbour. He heard the smart-sharp click of the cane against the bark of the trees. He heard the whisper it made on the grass, felt its thud against apples fallen on the earth. He learnt to hold the cane like an antenna, to trust the way it gave like bamboo so it would not throw him off. He learnt to understand its vibrations, the way it read objects for him.

Diane had sent him to secretarial college where he had learnt to touch-type. He sat, legs dangling from his chair, headphones on, a boyish blip in a row of grown girls. There, no one used blindfolds. You focused on watching the letters appear on the screen. A voice narrated the keyboard, drilling the fingers of each hand. Soon he could type like a professional. He could type so fast he mostly stopped using a pen. He worked up homework on his father's old Smith Corona. He liked the sound of the keys.

There is a group – all sitting together; one of them groaning in a soft monotone. The large, bespectacled woman in charge is skimming a paper. A paunchy man in a livid blue vest peers at her with bloodshot eyes. 'I'm sorry,' he says, rapidly blinking. 'I'm sorry for what I said earlier. I didn't mean it.'

An elderly woman ambles towards check-in, guided by a friend. The whites of her eyes show through thin, inverted crescents, gummy half-moons bordered by swollen lids.

For his first appointment, Sean had travelled with his mother from their small town to London by train. His face had been pressed to the glass. He saw the great domed roof of Paddington Station as they pulled in, stood small beneath it on the long platform, Diane tugging at his hand to move him along.

They found the hospital, but ate lunch in the park close by before going in. They sat on a bench they would revisit, overlooking a fountain surrounded by worn lion's heads with manes of melted stone.

He first met Max in the park. Max was there for an appointment. Max was with his mother, and when they entered the park they were holding hands. Sean could remember the smart clothes the mother wore, her buttoned gloves, and creamy skin. He didn't remember her name.

Max himself was the same age as Sean, but young-old. He was uneasy, expectant, seemed always to be bracing himself for bad news. Sean recalled the cautious, formal way he wanted to shake hands, and the neat parting in his hair, and the way he said Ull-ope instead of Hello.

Later, when they played, Max would stop suddenly. Sean would watch him reach out to test the air.

At lunchtime, a posse of young white-coats sweeps out of the clinic. Sean is still waiting and the room still packed. At the check-in desk the staff are chatting hem-lengths. One of them leans forward, hitching up her skirt.

Three children are racing up and down the corridors beside the seats. They are part of an extended family who are taking up a whole row, and who have come prepared with brown paper bags of tortilla chips and wraps. Both grandparents are handsome in feathered felt hats. Peruvian, perhaps. When the old man takes a handful of chips, he presses his wife's cheek very gently with one palm, and then holds one of them to her lips. The children stick their palms beneath the hand sanitiser, and then smack them hard together, giggling as they explode the foam.

*

Max.

If, at the start, they were in it together, the two of them, it was a promise established as much by their mothers as by themselves.

It wasn't chance that their consultations always fell on the same day. Co-ordinated visits meant the afternoons could be transformed into something else; an excursion, an adventure. As the boys explored, their mothers walked, and talked, and bolstered each other. Though their conditions were not the same, time for both was the big hope. There was no real treatment to be had.

For Sean there were only sunglasses, and vitamin A.

Diagnosis must have brought some relief to Max and his mother – to have a name to attach to the things that had been going on. Max was blind in one eye, and had hallucinations that came out of nowhere.

He was meant to keep a journal, to draw the visions out of the ether, to fix them somewhere more real, to make him less scared. He didn't want to keep a journal – perhaps it seemed like homework; he had a sketchbook instead.

The things Max saw.

There were cartoons: Bagpuss, Professor Yaffle. There were knights and dragons. His drawing was not bad, and anything he could not draw he cut out of magazines and pasted in.

'You see all this?' Sean had asked, in wonder.

Aged eight, Max was measured, uncertain – a small, stooped boy, his arms wrapped around his chest or held behind his back. With permission to play, with a companion at hand, he was self-conscious, stopping at intervals in their games to reach out and ask, 'Is there a wall?' At times he would shout, 'Leave me alone. Go away.' At times he would stop, his arms clamped to his sides, and simply stare.

He seemed baffled by friendship. At first he barely made eye contact. He would not talk about school. But he would always have the sketchbook with him and, while he never handed it over, he had a way of leaving it alone, so Sean would pick it up, and see. It was a form of silent agreement that they slipped into, without Sean really understanding what the agreement was.

Crowding the front of the book were the knights and dragons – these followed by cartoons. Closer to the middle there were patterns, all intricately drawn.

The back of the book Sean tried hard to forget. It was populated with grotesques: swollen-headed people with boggle-eyes and over-large teeth.

*

The woman next to Sean is explaining in bad English that her eyes are broken, or that she's worried they will be broken, or that an optician had told her she must take care not to break them, which is why she's here. She got here at eleven, says she heard the Peruvians have been here since eight. Sean thinks the woman is French. He doesn't ask; although here in New York, where origins are like credentials, perhaps she would not be offended.

One of the kids is cupping foam sanitiser: she moves carefully across the floor. The girl transfers the foam to her grandmother's hands, and rubs it in. When the job is done, the old woman reaches out to touch the child's face.

A Sikh in a grey turban circles the waiting room slowly.

*

Looking back, Sean could not say how many consultations each of them had. When the appointments fell away the four of them continued to meet – Max, Sean, Diane and Max's mother revisiting, over and over, the area that had become familiar.

In the streets, along the passageways that ran close to the hospital, there were places the boys believed were entirely their own: outside the hospital gates, the plaque for William Wallace, who had been hanged, drawn and quartered; across the square, the market where men had sold their wives; on the way to St Paul's, the memorial to Heroic Self Sacrifice, for those who had faced quicksand or runaway horses as they fought to help another.

At that time, Sean's condition was stable; in daylight he had no problems at all. For Max, the sketchbook seemed to help. He became less fearful, less apologetic. With Sean, he knew he had an ally in negotiating space – the sudden changes, the appearance of walls and fences that only he could see. He would ask if they really were there, and Sean would lead the charge through open space – across grass, or paving, or back and forth in the little park where they had first met, where long ago there had been jousts and tournaments.

They were friends, sure – but now, looking back, Sean could see that even from the start there were small things; small slights, small hurts.

Max had more than a label, in fact: he had a syndrome. Sean watched him, with time, reaching out with confidence and swiping at the air as if he knew there was really nothing there. The hallucinations became, by increments, a mark of distinction, a badge of honour. By the time they had known each other a year, Max seemed proud of the way his condition set him apart, as if he had a special gift.

'My visions,' he started to say.

At Smithfield Market one day, Sean had pointed to the roof. 'I see a dragon,' he said. There it was, crouched low, its tongue flicking in anger – wings raised, ready to launch. Max had followed his line of vision, and shrugged dismissively: 'So what?'

In his book, Max had sketched the stars and all the constellations – the sky at night. He drew a fish, a scorpion, a lion, and a charging bull. He drew a creature with a bow and arrow – half-man, half-beast.

'You see all that?' Sean asked.

Max eyed him sidelong. 'Everyone does.'

'Not me,' Sean shook his head.

Sean told Diane he never knew. All those creatures up there. Why hadn't she told him? He was bereft. 'I never knew,' he said. 'I don't see any of that.'

'Nobody does,' his mother told him – furious. 'Nobody sees any of that.'

All the same, Sean felt his own world was prosaic. His mother was pragmatic and assertive. There was no special treatment. She made sure that the things he saw were all dealt with, and explained.

Once, after a Halloween feast at a friend's house, he told her he had seen skulls lit from within, with haloes of light around them.

'Tell me again,' his mother said. 'Tell me exactly what you saw.' He stressed that he had seen their jaws dancing and gaping; he felt she was somehow missing the point. 'Haloes? You're seeing haloes?' she said, when he had finished.

He tried to tell her everyone had seen the sugar skulls that way, but she wanted to speak with the consultant. Haloes could be symptomatic, but lights could be adjusted. They were adjusted.

'You and me, Chick,' his mother said.

It wasn't envy, exactly, but if asked at that time, if given the choice, he would have traded places with Max. He would have wanted the constellations, and everything else that came with them.

Combing the lanes around the hospital he tried to draw their worlds together; to notice things. 'Look!' he would say. 'Do you see that?' On the gateway to the church of St Bartholomew-the-Great he pointed out heraldic shields and inside, columns of pale stone, wooden angels, winged beasts. The memorial plaque that once, it was said, wept real tears.

Max wasn't impressed. Sean felt his own lack.

Still he remembers the smell of incense in the church, the cloistered walkways, the high-quiet sound of the wind up above.

'The haloes have come back,' he told Diane.

When he was very small, they'd made a game, the two of them, of holding their breath: who could do it the longest, who could make it through tunnels in the car. When he cheated – when he pretended he could hold his breath two minutes and counting – she never let on that she knew. It was part of the set-up, part of the fun, allowing the lie.

Over the course of a week, he told her that the haloes were now with him even during the day; told her that they were like exploding suns, obscuring his vision.

One night, a sound he barely recognised: he heard her crying through the wall. It had not occurred to him that despite her busy practicality his mother may still feel hurt.

He never told her that he'd made it up – said instead that the haloes had vanished, almost overnight. She had taken him out for a special tea. She allowed him to choose both of their cakes. She sat across the table from him, watchful, tender, as he picked at the icing. He had never felt more ashamed.

'Don't you like it?' she'd asked.

There was no great drama. His falling out of touch with Max came about the way it often does with friendship. Time passes. Isn't that it? This is what he'd told himself over the years.

Max had become a feverish, tiring presence. If at the start there was unspoken agreement – they were in this together – for Sean that agreement had ended. At some stage, a call from Max ignored. Then silence.

At fifteen, Sean had received a card through the post from Max's mother: a small, neatly drawn announcement.

There was no mention of a service. No mention either of what had happened, though it was clear somehow that it was suicide. So brief, the announcement, and so careful.

Not long after this: the sketchbook. *He would want you to have it.*

On his first visit to New York, aged twenty-five, he had stood in the concourse at Grand Central Station, and looked up. He saw the sky at night and all the constellations. He saw those stars lit up.

He found a postcard of the ceiling for Diane. *I see the stars.* He bought a stamp, and found his way out on to the street. He found a postbox on a corner nearby.

He tore the postcard up.

*

The woman in the lemon blanket is telling a story to her daughters; she is imitating someone. 'But I don't *want* to stay in this apartment,' she says, in a whiny, nasal tone. 'I don't *want* to stay in this cramped-assed apartment.' She laughs loudly, as if it's the funniest thing she ever heard. 'But it is a cramped-assed apartment,' one of the girls says.

The door to the toilet swings open. Inside the Peruvian kids are clambering about, crazed with waiting.

The friend in whose apartment Sean has been staying is away on honeymoon. The apartment is not especially cramped-assed: Tom works for a hedge fund. For Sean it has been a chance to try it on for size for a few weeks. He has a string of interviews at another firm. He has been telling himself he is still young enough to make the move: he loves it here, he can see himself here, and in London he has no big relationship ties. His friends are all scattered about. His father is gone. His mother would surely want this for him.

Before Tom left, they spent an evening together at a summer screening in Bryant Park, the grass thronged with picnickers. The film was black and white. Something with Bette Davis. There was a soft, blue flow from the silver Airstream housing the projector. In the small side window the head of the projectionist would disappear and reappear as he moved about. At dusk the sky changed colour, took on a deep blue striated with rose. In the buildings on all sides Sean noticed the lights – thousands of them. The floors of a tower block straight ahead were blinking on and off in an irregular rhythm, like a code; four or five floors at once were light, then dark, light, then dark. The sky deepened. There were spontaneous bursts of clapping, and laughter: a good shared feeling. Close by, a woman was explaining the plot to a friend. All around, people were repeating the lines of the film as it played. 'Fasten your seatbelts,' they chanted loudly, all together, 'it's gonna be a bumpy night.' Sean noticed the Airstream then, and thought for a moment there was a fire. It was throbbing light into the dark. It was haloed. When he looked back at the screen it was blurred.

He had closed his eyes and listened: to the thrum of the buildings, the traffic, the voices, the cars breaking, the buses and trucks letting off steam, the shrill whining – somewhere – of an alarm, the frantic warble of police cars and ambulances.

When you heard it all around you it really was something.

On the subway home, the strip lights flared over ads for Caesar's, Atlantic City. *Routinely Spectacular Entertainment*, he read. *Ready. Set. Conquer. Live in the Moment.* The lights spat incandescence.

That night, in the apartment: helicopters, air conditioners. He couldn't sleep. He had stood a long while in the bathroom, with the lights dimmed, running his fingertips back and forth across the cool, smooth enamel of the sink. His heart was beating fast, and he thought he might be sick.

He had made his way out on to the street and walked, and found himself a diner, and sat, and watched. He had ordered a club sandwich and coffee. It was three in the morning. There was a comforting level of noise; the diner almost full. A female student with long dark hair down to her waist had been working on a paper in a booth beside the wall. A twitchy young man who was half-reading Nietzsche had been doing his best to catch her eye; he kept casting glances, folding the corner of the page he was on, and setting the book down, and looking at her, and then picking the book back up.

Sean felt in the diner he had stepped out of time: that this thing might not be happening. The lights were up. He could see fine. There were no haloes. Not around the lights over the counter. Not around the lights on the walls. Under his hands the silver tabletop was alive with fluid light that moved about, benign, each time he moved. He felt optimistic, even. At the counter a man said, 'This is the best coffee I ever had!'

After a while, the light hurt.

He hadn't said anything to Tom. He had stayed on in New York. There were things he could do to manage, and he could manage, at first. He had stuck to the plan.

So late now, perhaps, that no one's in a rush.

Young registrars hang around in doorways, lean against the doorframes, look vague and hopeful. 'Anything interesting?' they say. They are clean and well-kempt. Their skin probably smells of soap, or cologne. When they are not hopefully leaning, they skim along the corridors wanting to be seen to be doing, when now, at the end of the day, there is so little to be done.

Sean's registrar comes towards him in heavy black head-gear with compound eyes. After the registrar, the consultant looms, his hairless head like a large cannonball, his eyes lacking light or expression.

'Aha-aha, aha-aha, aha-aha,' he says. His breath smells sharply of peppermint.

They dilate Sean's eyes, to get a proper look.

Over dinner, before Bryant Park, Tom had told him about the blackout in Manhattan the year before. Smiling faces. Candlelit stores.

It was good times, Tom had said, until the water began to run out, and people started to smell for the lack of a shower. Tempers became frayed; the candlelit stores were no longer charming. Faces were semi-obscured. They could be things of beauty or terror. It all could turn on a dime.

The registrars are gathered. The consultant turns to one to them and asks his opinion.

The registrar looks blank, then wary, and then he flushes and says, 'I agree with you.'

'Oh?' the consultant says.

'I don't like it.'

Before coming to the clinic that morning, Sean had stood in St Patrick's up on Fifth Avenue, and had watched – high up, far off in that cathedral space of shadows – the stained glass and sunlight shoaling together, protean, patterning the walls with colour.

He had closed his eyes and looked for those colours.

He could still be here, he'd told himself. He could still get a job. He could still make the move.

'You're how old?' the consultant says to Sean.

'Forty.'

'Aha-aha.'

The registrars retreat. It is just the two of them now. The

consultant sets aside the headgear, and the paperwork, and then he turns back to Sean, appraises him fully.

'You've been told where this is going. Am I right?' he says. Sean nods. He had wanted to know, for sure.

He holds on in the clinic, waiting there in the rows of empty seats, alone now apart from the Sikh who stands quiet in a corner, smiling at anyone who happens to pass; alone now apart from the cleaner doing his rounds, emptying bins in the restrooms, wiping down the floor.

And then the Frenchwoman comes out through the double doors. She must be one of the last.

Like him, her eyes have been dilated. Her pupils are huge and black. She's laughing. An allergy, she says. She has to take steroid drops. 'I thought my eyes were broken. I thought something terrible,' she says. She drops into the seat next to his. Her vision is still blurred with the dilation. It's the first time she's had it done.

'It'll pass,' he tells her. He says he'll walk her to the subway.

Together they head for the door, waving goodbye as they go to the Sikh who says, 'All done?'

They make their way along the corridor, following the exit signs.

Outside the clinic, there is still sunshine, the buildings watery with light: those long summer days.

The shock of it is blinding. They have to stop to acclimatise.

★

Along with the stars, he will lose faces: that constellation of the familiar put out. His mother. His father. His friends. Himself.

He will try to locate himself through the keys of an old Smith Corona. He will do this even before finding a ribbon. He will rediscover the small ridged discs against his fingertips, will find the feel of it, the sound of it unchanged: this memory true.

He will need to rediscover the world through touch.

He will remember that when Max's blindness was getting worse – probably, actually, getting worse – he had made a request. Max had asked – awkward and solemn.

He will find he cannot recall the words Max used, but will understand it was a whole new pact he had been offered.

To trace the contours of a face. To feel the warmth of hands on his own.

But the friendship, by then, had not been something he wanted.

He had told Max, No.

'Hello. I'm Christopher,' she heard, and when she raised her head and opened her eyes there he was, right in front of her – his skinny ankles no more than a couple of inches from her face.

This was how it tended to happen. This was how the scenario played itself out.

She looked up. 'Hello,' she said. 'What's up, Christopher?'

'Do you want to play?' He presented the question – rather flat, a little wan – like a dish he had prepared that had turned out bland, and beige, and unappealing, so he wasn't necessarily expecting a positive response. She looked up, squinting, to the rest of him, and saw his body plastered with the sun cream his mother had applied, and the white cloth sun hat, the kind that babies wear with great floppy rims, and beneath it his pale face, the nose obliterated by factor 50. His eyes, large and blue and long-lashed, were glittering beneath the indignities that had been piled upon him, and his thin red lips were burning furiously.

She hauled her body to its feet.

'Lead on, Christopher.'

He gave her the loveliest smile, and then led the way towards the rock pools and the cliffs.

But of course this was not how it had happened, not how it had played itself out.

*

Later she would learn about alternatives, but that summer, that first time, Frankie had shuttled up and down the beach with pads, back and forth between the encampment her family had made close to the water, and the interminable queue for the loos. Accompanying her all the while was an ache deep in her pelvis, which made her grateful for the kick of heat coming from the sand beneath her feet.

That queue, over and over – bodies shuffling inch by slow inch, limbs lazy in the sun, arms swatting listlessly at flies, like the tails of cows. The stink of urine. The wet sand gritty and slippery against the concrete underfoot. Then the toilet more like a shower; the white porcelain stained and chipped with an uninviting platform for each foot, and filthy overflow – including her own – from the bin. Squatting there, through the wide gap underneath the stall door, Frank would inspect the flip-flopped feet that were lined up and waiting.

She had felt stranded wherever she went: stranded in the water, knowing each time she swam there was a risk she would humiliate herself on her way out; stranded and oddly solitary as she made the quick change, under cover of her towel, into the relative safety of padded knickers and shorts; stranded as she marched up the beach to the queue, past those who were flat out and happy and careless, when she was not.

Standing in the shallows, the small waves washing over her feet, she had looked back towards the mound of towels and bags and picnic things surrounding her parents, who lay reading, or sleeping, or watching as her brothers dug a moat around their castle in the sand. She had felt hot and stupid in her clothes.

'Frankie, take off your shirt,' her mother had teased. But she couldn't.

She hated the way her brothers shook her off – the look of absence in their eyes when they rested on her. She hated that.

Instead of running around as she would usually do, or diving off rocks, Frank spent time sitting and watching instead. First she would look for her brothers, and then she would let her gaze trail right along the beach, where perfect surf was coasting in, where bodies hurled themselves about, ecstatic.

She watched as down the beach a woman and her son arrived and started setting up camp. The woman – sallow-looking – fussed over the boy. She plastered him with cream; it didn't look like fun. The boy picked his way towards the water, and stood gazing out, his feet barely wet. He did a little dance there, at the water's edge, and then turned to look for his mother.

Frank studied her own parents – her mother on her belly, deep in her book, her father, cross-legged, picking at a hang-nail on his toe.

There were others she remembered like pieces on a chess board.

She remembered a man – white-haired, slim, and wearing spectacles, wire-rimmed – who held the hand of a girl playing in the sea. Years later she could picture him, carried an image of him in her mind, as if it mattered.

She remembered another younger man on her route up the beach, lying in a pair of yellow Speedos so tight she had to force herself to look away: his skin slick, his thighs prominent, his body, even at rest, in a state of readiness – tense and compact.

She remembered the two teenage girls who were closer to the spot her family had claimed, halfway between the water and the ridge of seaweed marking high tide, far from the fuss at the top of the beach – the back and forth, the queues, the booths for food. They too had chosen the sand that was firm, that was good for digging and striated with shells – the broken fragments smoothed by the sea, the larger clams and cuttlefish prized by Frank's brothers – though mostly all they did was lie there talking about nights out, past and future.

She could remember too, beside the rocks to the left of the girls, close to the cliffs, the woman dressed only in bikini bottoms squatting in the sand, skin scorched to mahogany and wizened with age, breasts flat against her chest.

Frank had watched her father playing chess often. The board in their living room alcove was equipped with handsome resin figurines. They were the Lewis Chessmen: the king stunned; his sullen, cogitative queen with one hand resting on her cheek and looking – Frank's mother said – as if she'd had one bitch of a week; the knight with a cloak draped in perfect folds over his steed; the steed the most contented of the lot, Frank always thought, with a very satisfying, perfectly straight fringe.

Her father had tried to teach her. She would sit in the armchair across from him, planted sideways and almost inverted with the soles of her feet pressed flat against the wall. He told her more than once that she had things the wrong way round: she insisted each time on retracing her steps to get her bearings, always making a mental journey back to the start. 'Look ahead!' he would urge. But back she would go, over and over, to the beginning, where everything was clear, and where the figurines were neatly lined up in a row.

That day, on the beach, she had felt something in motion, the main players having already made moves. She could find no clear beginning, and yet the powerful feeling remained, long afterwards – if only she could.

The older woman had seemed familiar. Frank felt she had seen her before; found herself pondering the face scored with lines, the limbs thin and loose-skinned.

'Frank,' her mother had said. 'You're staring.'

She couldn't place her, couldn't think where it had been. 'I'm not.'

She fell back on her towel, and then flipped herself over so her face was pressed hard into the damp, salt-smelling cloth. Behind her eyelids she saw explosions – fireworks in orange and blue spinning trails through the dark.

Close by, a girl had been going on to a friend. It was impossible not to hear every word; as she warmed to her theme her voice became loud and hard – relentless. The theme was vomit. Behind her closed lids Frank had visions of the girl painting a car, a hallway, and then a kitchen, with great sticky lumps of the stuff.

'Ice cream anyone?' Frank's father had said.

For Frank, the voice had conjured someone stocky and ugly, so when she opened her eyes and located the girls it seemed impossible that the words belonged to them – both slim and attractive, one a redhead, the other with a dark, glossy mane. They had been older than Frank by only a few years, but seemed so sure of themselves. She could remember their legs flicking up and down as they lay on their towels, and the way they changed position for an even tan, like old hands, and the ritual they made of comparing white marks under bikini straps.

Suddenly there was the small boy, in front of the girls. What could have possessed him? She couldn't hear what he said, but they shrieked with laughter.

He stood there a moment, looking at them, before moving off. A few feet away he stopped and seemed to be taking stock. He started making his way towards her.

'No,' she breathed. 'No. No. No. No. No.'

She fell forward on her towel, flat out, pretending to sleep.

'Hello,' a voice said. 'I'm Christopher.'

'Hello Christopher,' she heard her father say, agreeably. 'What can we do for you?'

'I've come to play.'

'Frank!' her father called out, as if she were some distance away, or in her room at the top of the stairs.

'No.'

'Frankie!'

She could sense him standing there, right at the edge of her towel. Slowly, she propped herself up on one elbow, and shielded her eyes from the sun with her hand.

His toes were curled tight, all together, his pale feet smeared with sunscreen, and clotted with sand. He stood there bravely, small shoulders back. It was as if, for that moment, his whole body were on pause, as if he were holding his breath.

Frank tried hard to imagine hauling herself up but everything in her felt heavy; a great weight was bearing down. It was impossible.

'I'm sorry Christopher,' she said.

He squinted through his disappointment, blinked in the sun, and walked away.

According to her mother she would, in time, feel nostalgic for those days – the way her body flushed itself out like clockwork, with such force, with those torrents of blood. But that day she groaned with hot rage and thrashed her legs about in the sand.

'It hurts,' she said, into her towel, kicking her feet, trying to shake off the heavy ache creeping down into her thighs. 'I have to go again,' she said, sitting up and rifling, furious, in her bag.

'Oh Frank.' This was her mother. 'Are you sure? You've only just been.'

'You're exhausting to watch,' her father said. 'Just leave it be.'

'How can she leave it be?'

'If you were in Nepal they would kick you out of the house.'

Frank glared at her father.

'You're a pollutant.'

'Thom. For God's sake,' her mother said.

He shrugged. He was enjoying himself. 'They wouldn't let you prepare food, either.'

'Fine.' Frank threw the wad of pads she had ready in her hand on to her towel, not bothering to hide them away. 'Fetch your own ice cream.'

It was good to get away from the sweltering sand and on to the rocks where there was a breeze. In the shadow of the cliffs it was cool underfoot.

She found a place to stand on a large, smooth rock with a perfect indentation for her feet. She slotted herself in and looked back towards the beach, which was warped now by the hazy heat. Mirages, slippery like mercury, appeared and disappeared, rolling their silver along folds in the sand that could not possibly be there. It all looked like a picture on paper that someone had taken and crumpled in their fist and then released, producing odd ridges and troughs, a relief changing shape as the paper relaxed, a slow metamorphosis startled here and there by odd spasms – the sudden surge of a kite, the spume of a cresting wave, the panicked flap of a pyjama-striped windbreak.

Standing there, looking back towards her parents, she tried to assess how long it would take her to make it to them, and to supplies, and then on to the toilets up at the top of the beach. The memory of an attempted swim was fresh with humiliating detail: those rivulets of watery blood coursing down her legs. She hadn't even noticed. She had been standing on her beach towel shivering with pleasure from the salty cold, when her mother had said, '*Frank.*'

From her rock she could see her father, on his feet, arms crossed, looking out towards the water – a pose she recognised from the lecture theatre, where as a child she had once been allowed to sit and watch. She could see the girls in their bikinis, ankle-deep in the water, long hair snatched up by the wind. She could see the older man reading to the little girl up above the line of seaweed, and Christopher in his floppy sun hat dragging a spade in solitary circles in the sand. 'Only boring people—' she mouthed. And then, 'Only boring people, Christopher, get bored,' she said, parroting Ms Wilson her head teacher.

Hot and dizzy, she sat on the smooth stone, her legs stretched in front, palms flat. She closed her eyes and felt the breeze that was coming off the water licking at her face. Behind her lids something plummeted, fast and dark and heavy – as if all the movement on the beach had found its way inside to merge with the exhaustion she felt pulling her down. She lay back, the noise of people – the hordes, their screams – fading to something distant.

Years later, she would try to describe the feeling to a boyfriend who wanted to know what it was like; who found it all *fascinating*; who used the word 'menses'; who would ask her to set it out over brunch in King's Cross, even knowing that people could hear. She would find herself embarrassed on his behalf for being so po-faced, for being such a fucking try-hard.

'You'll never know,' she would say, mashing her eggs Benedict with her fork and slowly shaking her head, all the while willing some laughter, longing for more of a sense of humour from him.

But he would insist.

'This is what it feels like,' she would say, as they sat hemmed in at their table, couples in their faces on either side. 'It feels like a hand is reaching inside you and twisting until you double over, thighs aching, burning. Between the legs: rawness, heat, and blood, and lust, and fear, and disgust, and shame, and humiliation.'

'Eat up,' she would say, as he picked at his food.

He would be disappointed, even hurt; would shake his head slowly; would say, as they settled their bill, that she wasn't the person he'd hoped for; would say she had a hard edge that he couldn't fathom.

It was the sound of rock on rock that woke her. She raised her head and opened her eyes, brushing vaguely with her forearm at moisture collected around her mouth.

She saw him, like a vision at the water's edge, moving slowly towards her. He didn't have his floppy hat on, but wore goggles, and yellow flippers, oversized. He was luminously pale, and wide-eyed, with every movement halting.

He was a thing of awkward beauty, a strange bird newly hatched.

'Oh, Christopher,' she said, half under her breath.

A rush of warmth from her belly and she was laughing. She was delighted. He seemed to her lit up. She was surprised at the feeling that caught in her throat.

She watched as he proceeded, head craning forwards and downwards, goggled eyes trained on each foot as he tried to take a step that proved each time almost impossible.

'Your flippers are too big,' she murmured.

She watched him as he stopped and pulled the goggles up on to his forehead, and looked about in an assessing kind of way. She watched as he poked his head forward, goggle-free, and tried again. He would reach a point of no return, perform a pirouette on the end of each flipper as he tried to lever it out of the wet sand.

'Your flippers are too big.'

She let out a sigh of relief when he changed tack and shuffled backwards – now something closer to a crab – and actually, finally, got his feet properly wet. Knee high in the water he re-secured his goggles, and folded himself so he was doubled over and peering down beneath the surface of the sea.

Again, Frank heard rock striking against rock. She tried to follow the sound but it came in bursts, sporadic, and the way noise was carried about on the breeze it was hard to tell.

She saw then, scrambling on rocks close by, where seaweed was pasted in dark seams underfoot, the woman: topless, shrunken, her hair hanging matted to her neck. She must have been sixty at least, but along her hairline, running sideways and framing her face, there was a plait – the kind of thing schoolgirls had.

Frank understood now what it was she had heard, saw the woman squat to attack a citadel of limpets, saw her hacking at them, over and over, with a rock. When she set the rock down, and the sound stopped, she brought the broken shells to her mouth, one by one, and sucked the tender creatures out.

Awful.

The woman was spider-like, scrawny. A string of weathered shells, like little skulls, were slung around her neck. More of them garlanded her hair. Hollow-eyed and freakish. One of Frank's father's favourites. They had seen her at the British Museum. She appeared half-starved, and voracious: the great goddess in the form of an old hag. From collarbones down to empty breasts her ribs were scored across her chest.

Standing to go, Frank knew she was in trouble; a clot of dark blood had somehow worked its way into the open from between her legs. A change of position? The movement to stand? It didn't matter now. It had fingered its mark on her upper thigh – a stamp, black and fibrous.

Movement. What looked to her like seaweed bothered by the wind. Again she saw that scraggy, salt-tangled hair. She felt herself to be swaying up on her rock, and dizzy. She was frightened. She tried to plot a route back to her parents, whatever the humiliation involved. She turned at a sound close by, and found those pitted eyes fixed on her from only a few feet away, a smile on the woman's lips. Everything went silent. She felt her insides twist.

And then the pieces on the chessboard moved all at once, no rules to their game.

Frank would remember this moment later, when, aged thirty-five, she lost control of her car on a bend, watched her hands sit impassively on the wheel as the car ran off the road and lost its hold on the earth, as it found the tipping point beyond which there is no return, falling, rolling then in a movement of some grace until it flipped and settled in the shallow waters of a saltmarsh. The paralysis she would feel, the separation from the scene as she hung there suspended by her seatbelt, the world upside down and brackish water sidling in through the open window of the car.

She had simply watched it unfolding: a story over which she had no control.

She saw the man in yellow Speedos striding out into the water, all sure-footed muscularity. He passed the girls, who were leaping over the smallest of the waves. He broke into a run, his legs ploughing the water, and then – arms arrowed forward – he pierced the surface and disappeared. She thought in that moment to look for Christopher, but was distracted by the sight of the older man – the man earlier with the small girl – who was alone now, and walking fast, running even, seemed to be running towards Frank. Frank looked for the little girl and could not find her. She caught movement on the rocks closest to the sand. She saw that the man was running not to her but to the end of the beach, where the scrawny woman was now standing up to her knees in the water – all leather, all skin and bones, the string of shells hanging down from her neck.

But it was not even to her that he was running, Frankie realised, at last. He was not running to her.

It was to Christopher, who was bobbing adrift in the shallows, the tender skin of his back white in the sun.

THE ISLAND

I

Underwater, she keeps her eyes open. In the shallows there, the sunlight is live and lighting up small particles of what must be the white sand disturbed by her feet and hands when intermittently she moves. She tries not to move. She tries to hold her body still under the water so that she can feel the pull to and fro as she watches out for fish. She should swim further out, she would see more there, but she doesn't.

Bringing her head above the water now she sees him on the beach. He is flat out, on his back. He looks toned, muscular, which would make him pleased. He is not moving. The beach is slanted enough to make it look as though he might slide downwards, towards her, on the soft sand. But he doesn't. He looks impossibly still. He looks as though someone has given him a shot of something – maybe something for cattle.

The beach is slanted up towards the line of palm trees that, with the white sand, look like the line of palm trees you would imagine on a dream beach, the ideal version. It was what they had been promised.

II

They had been woken by drilling on their first morning. They were digging up the area in front of the hotel. Quite apart from the noise, the room was shaking. There was a pile of rubble as high as a car, men milling about. She had pulled the curtains shut, groaned, let out a scream as she stamped her foot like a child, and then gone into the bathroom, slamming the door.

'What?'

'I want to kill someone,' she shouted.

When she was out of the shower and dressed she stood over him. He lay with the sheet pulled over his head. 'Get up.' His face appeared, puffy and vulnerable with jet lag. He looked lost and it made her want to shake him. 'Come on,' she said.

They had been told it was safest to go to the market with someone local, but they hadn't: Frank hated the idea of being chaperoned as a foreign woman here, being told not to feel safe. She took the precaution, only, of letting the woman at reception know where they were going. She had been irritated by the way the woman raised her eyebrows and made her mouth into a silent O. She had walked out of the lobby at a pace, her flip-flops slapping the Formica tiles with force.

Euan insisted on wearing a money belt. The guidebook said you shouldn't carry cameras and you shouldn't have evidence of a wallet or a purse. Euan had fallen asleep the night before with the guidebook lying open on his chest, as if he were trying to absorb absolute truths through his skin. She had thought to throw it out of the window, or hide it, but he would have been upset. It would not have been a good start to the trip. She had also bitten her tongue against the impulse to tell him that everyone knew about money belts. It was the first place they would look. It was not hard to lift up a tee shirt, flick open a blade. Before leaving the hotel she had stuffed some money into her bra, but not much.

At the market, fish were sold fresh from the boats. It was in a village at the end of a beach not far from town. She had seen pictures of the houses before – looking precarious at low tide, on stilts. The homes were wooden-slatted, painted in muted blues and pinks.

It was high tide when they arrived. Fish were laid out on stalls, in neat rows, or hung like bunches of bananas, strung together. Women stood, talking, waiting for business. Frank stopped at a stall where thin silvery fish were banked up. She smiled at the woman behind the stall, who beamed back, betel juice running red through her teeth.

Euan got into an improvised conversation; he was waving his arms in the air. Before coming away, he had studied the glossary at the back of the guidebook, hoovering up words so he could point at something and name it.

She walked on a way until she came to the end of the stalls and the boarding gave way to water. She looked out. Through her sunglasses everything took on a kind of purple glaze. With one hand she raised them and squinted out across the bay. The water was brilliant with sunlight. Beneath the surface, beneath her feet, it transformed into roving beams, kaleidoscopic.

The first time she had met Euan, in a bar, she was rude to him – but they had still gone home together.

They had ended up in the shower. He had flipped her around so that her face was pressed against the tiles. Her jeans had taken a while. They were wet and heavy and clung. As he tugged at them they pulled at her skin. He wouldn't let her turn around to help him. When she was naked, her knees and hipbones and nipples pressed against cold tile, she waited for what would happen next. His hands held her arms above her head; his palms – flat and warm – pinioned her wrists. She could feel him against her lower back, and when his hands slid down her body, taking in her upper arms, her shoulders, her armpits, her ribcage, her waist, she had been ready, poised.

'You have a filthy mouth,' he had said. The observation was tonally neutral.

She had let out a half-formed laugh. But she was uncertain – wondered if she had misjudged who she'd gone home with.

He had directed the showerhead – hot against her neck, the crook of her elbow, the back of her knees. He used the soap like a pumice stone against the skin on her arms, her legs.

When he was done, he stood back and surveyed his work. Her skin felt raw and flushed.

He threw her a towel. 'I'm going to make us some coffee,' he said, and left.

She had stood there awhile in the bath. The air was thick, the mirror misted, the door ajar. She could hear him – the clatter of the coffee tin, the kettle coming to life. As the fug cleared she saw her reflection over the sink – the startled look in her eyes, her ruddy cheeks, hair pasted in strands across her forehead.

He did pull-ups every day on the gym bars in the park across from his flat. He had a book by his bed of exercises for the healthy male. He took vitamin supplements.

The second time they met he punched a guy in a bar. The guy had been groping her. She hadn't yet decided what she was going to do about that. Euan had damaged the man badly enough for there to be blood. They had run. 'I could have handled that,' she said, as they headed down into the Tube. At his flat she had scrutinised his fist for cuts and bruising; they had both started laughing as if they were high. He had snagged her legs somehow with his own and walked her backwards across the floor.

He wasn't her kind of person at all. She often felt she had wandered into someone else's story.

'Don't jump,' somebody said from close by, from right behind her. It wasn't Euan.

She let her sunglasses drop into place and slowly turned around.

The man was wearing a white tee shirt and pale linen trousers rolled up to the knees. He was tall and athletic looking; lucky in his body.

'I wasn't going to,' she said.

A look of amusement was playing on his face. 'I didn't think you were. I wanted to talk.'

She could not see past him. He was tall enough for his frame to obscure the walkway, the market. She could not see Euan. Presumably Euan could not see her.

'Why did you want to talk?' She focused on keeping her voice strong.

The man laughed. 'Relax,' he said. He held up his hands to display empty palms, and then reached into the pockets of his trousers and pulled them inside out. Finally he yanked his tee shirt up to his ears to reveal only smooth, dark skin before letting it drop again.

'I didn't mean that,' she said. Although of course she did.

'You should have done. I have back pockets too.' He looked at her straight-faced for a second before reaching around and pulling out a packet of tobacco.

As he rolled a cigarette he shifted position and Frank saw the stalls flash into view. Euan was comparing the colour of his forearm with the forearms of the women behind the stall.

'I'm Pete,' the man said.

'Francesca.'

He offered her the cigarette. When he passed it to her for a moment their fingers touched. She put the cigarette between her lips and waited for him to bring the lighter in, then took a drag, nodding that it was lit. The paper tasted of sugar. Mixed with the tobacco it was a good taste. 'It's sweet,' she said. 'It's good.'

He finished rolling his own, lit it, and then turned fully towards her. Once again she was hidden by his frame.

'Let me take you somewhere,' he said. He let his eyes flicker over her face for a moment. 'I know a place. It's perfect.'

She smiled slowly. She looked away from him, down at the water.

'Nowhere's perfect,' she said.

'Believe me. White sand. Palm trees.'

'There's a lot of that about.'

'Not like this,' he said.

She remembered, then, flying in low over the harbour, her face pressed to the window. She looked up; she met his gaze.

Euan appeared out of nowhere and said, 'Hey. What?' The interrogative hung in the air. She could see him eyeing the cigarette in her hand, but he didn't say anything about that – not then. Instead, he put his arm around her shoulders. 'My wife,' he said. '*Meri*. Maybe we should get you that ring.'

Pete was smiling. Frank felt something in her twist.

'Plot spoiler,' Euan whispered.

She had it coming. On the flight out she would have liked to talk – but he had watched *The West Wing*, non-stop. A few hours in, sick of being ignored, she had pulled one of his headphones away from his ear. 'The president has MS.'

'No. No. No,' he had said.

'Actually, this man was offering to take us to this place he knows. Right? Pete?'

Pete raised his eyebrows – surprised, amused, she couldn't tell. But he nodded.

'What's so special about this place?' Euan asked.

'It's beautiful,' she said. Euan's arm stayed where it was. She felt the weight of it on her.

They stood there a moment in silence, then, the three of them. She kept a level gaze on Pete. Look at me, she willed him.

He moved from one foot to the other. His eyes became guarded now, and he was looking past them, away from them, for a route out of this.

Frank didn't want to be discarded. 'And I was going to ask him, have you done this before?' He turned to her. 'Have you?' she said. A wry smile. 'Yes,' he said. 'I have.'

She had his attention – but also the feeling that she was being mocked. She felt a kick of anger. 'We'd have it all to ourselves. Right?' she said.

Pete nodded again.

She shrugged off Euan's arm and took a step forward, reaching into her bra for cash. 'Okay. How much? Do I haggle?' She knew exactly how it sounded.

Something altered in Pete's gaze, and closed off. 'You can haggle if you want, but the price is fixed.'

The deal was that he would leave them on the island for one night, with supplies; they would be the only ones. He would take them early in the morning by boat.

III

She walked up the beach towards Euan and threw herself down in the sand.

'My head is spinning,' she said. 'It's like I've been drinking.'

The sky above her twisted and warped. A lightning shudder like a shoal of tiny fish passed through her chest.

Euan propped himself up on one elbow and looked down at her. 'It's probably the tide. It does that. You notice it most when you swim underwater.'

'Does what?'

'Creates currents.'

'How do you have this information?'

When they had set off the sun was already hot, the surface of the harbour water viscous in the light. She had imagined it warm beneath the feet, giving slightly like mud.

Pete had gestured them over, guiding them down steps to the boat where another, older man was at the helm, a mongrel pup at his feet. The man looked towards them, impassive, sizing them up. When they were seated Pete asked for the rest of the money and the man let out a long, low whistle at their wad of cash. Frank shrugged as if to say – we know what we're doing, we want this.

They sat waiting as Pete readied the boat. Euan was staring at his feet. He hadn't wanted to get up; had slept until the last moment. A flake of the croissant he had grabbed as they left the hotel was attached to his upper lip. Pete was talking all the while with the man, but their conversation was not in English.

'How far is it?' she asked, as they set off. Pete was coiling the rope that had tethered them to land and didn't hear, or didn't answer if he had. Euan was trailing one arm out of the side of the boat. The man at the helm had one hand on the tiller, while with the other he rolled a cigarette. 'How long will it take?' she asked. The man laughed at her, gold flashing in-between his teeth. The boat sped up. '*Longwe liklik,*' he said, and the hand holding the cigarette danced, dipping up and down in the breeze.

The man ignored her then. For the duration of the journey his eyes were fixed steadily ahead, or on Pete and the pup at his feet. It was only at the drop-off on the beach that he again paid her any notice. When he reached out to shake her hand she had instinctively smiled, but from within his grip, which was firm, she felt the pressure of the single finger he had separated to push, wriggling, obscene, into the soft skin of her palm. She had felt herself flush, embarrassed, transparent as a child. Laughter broke out of him, and the glint once more of gold. By the time she had recovered herself, and thought to ask when they were going to be picked up, the men were back in the boat, facing the bay. Their voices were raised, Pete leaning towards the man to hear as he revved the engine.

She had once been told by a friend who had been to a dream beach that underneath that perfect sand, horny, spiked crabs lay in wait for your feet: razor sharp, dangerous. When they had watched the boat disappear – its trail of spume, the small waves fanning out – she was standing on white sand sprinkled with tiny shells, like baby teeth.

Euan had sunk on to his knees.

His clothes were at his feet, his arms above his head. He turned to her and grinned, and then did a victory dance, running wide naked circles over the beach. He brought his knees up high, and flapped his arms like chicken wings.

Seeing him like that – so stupidly happy – she remembered the weekend they had gone to the coast, to a seaside town in England, for a change of scene. Their skin was pale for lack of summer. They were tired and a little frayed, both of them, at the start, but that weekend was perhaps the most fun they had ever had.

Mostly, they had kicked about the town, aimless like teenagers with nowhere to be. They had laughed at the décor displayed in photos outside the Hotel Europa, the faded candy-striped sofas and beds. They had found themselves lodged beside the sea wall, drunk on vodka, eating a *CELEBRATION!* sponge cake from a cardboard box, listening to the hiss and drag of water on shingle. They had propped themselves up against the wall to enjoy the warmth of the sun, but in no time were covered by hordes of black bugs, and had retreated away from the shore, ending up slumped on a bench with an abandoned For Sale sign beside them, clumps of soil attached to its base.

Later, they had crashed a wedding – caught sight of the lights close to the dunes and scrambled over the grass. A glowing jellyfish replete with tentacles, the marquee was throbbing light into the pooling dark, small figures wandering in and out. She had watched as Euan, unsteady at first, swaying a little, but upright nonetheless, made his way towards the bright opening. The pulse of music. She caught up and heard him snigger as someone tripped over a guy rope and swore.

They ate more cake, wedding cake, watching the dancing. Euan was hyped up.

'Watch me,' he said. And she had watched as he crossed the dance floor in a crablike movement, half-walking, half-dancing, but with the confidence of someone who just doesn't care. She watched him sidle up to the bride, wheel her round and wrap his arms about her with drunken affection.

And then he was back, grabbing Frank's hand and yanking her after, fast, in-between the rows of seats – past the long tables, the floral arrangements, and the scattered aftermath of the wedding feast: the crumpled napkins, the red wine pooling around an upset glass, the brown stains from the main course, the sugared almonds tied up in little baggies with ribbons plundered now by small children on the prowl.

They swam – waded into the water fully clothed.

It was freezing. They were standing waist deep, and he was very still. 'What?' she said. Her teeth were chattering. She was sobering up fast. It was time to go.

'What I would like to see now,' he had said, 'would be fireflies.'

'You don't mean fireflies,' she said.

'Yes, I do.'

'You mean phosphorescence,' she said, 'on the water.'

'Maybe that's what you would want. But let's not get things mixed up. Fireflies,' he'd said, 'over the water. Like little stars.'

Pete had given them a large cool box and a couple of holdalls. They set up camp at the top of the beach; laid a driftwood fire ready, slung hammocks between the trees.

And then they sat side by side in the warm sand looking out to sea.

'Where would we be,' Frank said. 'Where would we be if we just kept swimming in a straight line from here?'

'I don't know,' he said.

When they had left the market the day before, they had found a bar in town, and holed up drinking South Pacific beer: at the table next to theirs – all together, like in a joke – a volcanologist, an ornithologist, and an anthropologist. They were on an informational cruise. They had come from the National Museum, where they had been taking in masks and penis gourds.

'My dad was an anthropologist,' Frank had told them.

'Why would you travel all the way here,' the ornithologist had said, 'to just lie on a beach?'

Frank drew with one finger in the sand, but it wasn't anything, this thing she was drawing; it wasn't a word, or an animal, or anything at all.

'I'm going for a swim,' she said. 'Are you coming?'

'Uh-uh,' Euan said. He was flat out, already half asleep.

There was a woman Frank had read about, who tried to swim from Florida to Cuba. She swam through shark-infested waters. Through waters chock full of jellyfish. Through currents that could, any moment, sweep her away. This woman was also a motivational speaker. This woman believed in pursuing your dreams. Last time Frank checked she still hadn't succeeded – which made Frank sad, but also a little pleased.

She drifted in the shallows. She watched him lying there on the beach.

That weekend by the sea had been his idea, or maybe hers, she wasn't sure, but the concept was escape: escape from the city, escape towards a change of perspective, escape to the cold, flat waters of the east.

From the station they had dragged their cases behind them, up a road lined with low-rise housing, which would look to be the wrong road if it weren't the only one. And then evidence of life: the cash machine, the newsagent, the half-empty bakery, advertising in looping cursives, personalised celebratory cakes. A little further on, an outdoor roller disco: Freddie Mercury playing and teenagers clinging to each other in the small enclosure under a grey sky; giddy like lambs, limbs staccato, erratic.

It had been the most fun they had had. They had roamed the streets, looking in on other people's lives. She had watched him dancing with the bride: the pleasure on his face, his stupid, lovely smile. He had come back to her and taken her hand, flipped it over – fervently kissed the middle of her palm. They had run fast between the tables, the two of them. She had thought, perhaps this is it.

They walked the beach from one end to the other, right along the line of palms. Frank kept to the shade, while Euan walked a few feet from her, determined to remain in the full punch of sun. He said he wanted, when they got back, to look like he'd been away.

They found no paths leading inland, away from the beach. No sign of a single trail. They stood looking into a mass of tangled vegetation. Above them, great fronds of palm moved slow motion in the heavy air, in the almost-breeze.

The heat was prickling Frank's skin. Turning, she saw the water of the bay – sheet silver; flat and calm and inviting.

'What are we doing?' she said.

Perhaps he hadn't heard. Perhaps he was asleep.

'What are we doing?' she said again.

She was standing over him, dripping.

They had gone to visit his mother. There was china with rosebuds on the table. There were sandwiches – white bread with the crusts cut off. His mother's hair had been set for the occasion. Frank could see he was showing her something that meant a lot.

Not long after this, they were married.

When the fire was going, and the monster prawns they would eat were speared and suspended, Euan reached into the cool box, winking at her.

'Frankie says . . . ,' he said.

He pulled out the beer, cracked open a can for her, and a can for him. He took a swig – 'Result,' he said – and then exhaled loudly.

She dreamt of a crab in her sleep – it was gigantic, its legs went on forever. They were all over her, spiny bristles caught in her jumper, snagging the wool. She woke in a sweat trying to pull the jumper off.

'What if they don't come back?'

She had got out of her hammock. She was standing next

to his. She was pushing him awake with her hands. 'What if they don't come back?'

'Of course they will.' His voice was flat. 'Go back to sleep.'

'How do you know that? You don't know that.'

She walked towards the water, went in up to her ankles, and then to her knees. The moon was bright and the stars were powdered in a great band above her. She should love it all.

The noise from the undergrowth: those oversized cicadas, and frogs, and lizards, and snakes, all bleating at her in the dark.

She woke to the sound of the surf.

Euan was squatting close to the water's edge. 'Look,' he said.

It was a fish – ultramarine blue, a colour siphoned from the sea. It was circling a pool. The spines on its back gave it a hip mohican. It had charcoal fins. At centre its eyes were deep holes, but around the eyes were tiger striped bands of soft blue and sepia brown, angled so they narrowed towards the nose, giving it a look that seemed to her considered, appraising.

Frank turned to Euan smiling, and thankful, but he had gone.

She stayed, watching the fish orbit, balletic, its scales glimmering in the light. Along the length of it, rippled in with the deeper blue, and dabbed tribal around its dark eyes and out towards its gills – a luminescent white-blue.

Euan reappeared at her side. He scooped his hands together and shovelled them deep into the watery sand beneath the fish. He lifted it.

'What are you doing?' she said.

He made his way with the fish up towards the trees at the top of the beach. She was walking alongside, trying to keep up.

He set it down close to the fire, which was smoking, revived. The fish lay on its pile of wet sand, fins flat, gulping for air; on either side, the sticks that they'd used for the prawns the night before.

Euan took the fish in his hands and whacked its head against the base of the nearest palm. He had not killed it – the fish was still moving in his hands. He came back to the fire, knelt down, took up one of the sticks – long and thin – and then forced it in through the fish's mouth.

THE ICE CREAM SONG IS STRANGE

FLIGHT

It is not usual for Morris to travel economy. The proximity of his body to that of his neighbour is alarming. He can smell her even when his face is turned away. He can hear her eat.

He arrives wretched with tiredness. The weather is not on his side, but he knows all about jet lag and what has to be done and so heads off with things to see and do to keep him up and out until it is time – Japanese time – to go to bed. His suitcase is small and portable. He has only ever travelled with cabin baggage.

The ticket machines for Tokyo's transport system are baffling; the option for English does not get him any closer to understanding which buttons need to be pressed. When eventually he seems to be edging a step closer to clasping a ticket in his hand, the part of the machine that should take notes refuses his, and he has to start the whole thing over.

He takes a cab.

The museum that he has settled on for the afternoon is open, though save for one temporary exhibit all the galleries are closed. If he spoke Japanese maybe he would have understood this before buying his ticket.

He spends some time moving between floors, just to confirm that the door to every room is barred, and then plants himself in the corridor housing the temporary exhibit. He does not bother reading the oblong of text on the wall, which he can see is written in both Japanese and English – too little, too late, he thinks. Instead he walks anti-clockwise around the exhibit, wondering if his instinct is correct or whether he should be starting at the other end.

It is some kind of pictorial story about men pursuing a beast. The beast has been eating the women, or raping the women, or both. The men catch the beast. The beast is decapitated and his giant head paraded about. The same story seems to be told over, many times, in a succession of glass cabinets. The beast is consistently revolting; its head swollen and distorted, its eyes bugging, its teeth slavering. When he has had enough of the beast he moves on.

The Zen garden is closed due to inclement weather and he stands for a moment at a window looking out at the drizzle forming never-ending circles on the surface of the pond.

He works his way through the postcards in the museum shop, row after row, scanning exhibits he is not allowed to view. He can't think why he would buy anything or who he would be buying for. When it is time for the museum to close he has no desire to go, but the shop attendants efficiently corral the customers towards the door, bowing as they do. Grey electronically controlled security screens are coming down. The lights inside are being dimmed.

On his way out of the museum he makes a stop at the bathroom. He takes his time. Although there is no need for discretion – no one is there to hear him as he settles on the heated toilet seat – he pushes the button that activates the sound of flushing water. A sign informs him that the noise will last twenty seconds. After twenty seconds he pushes it again. He could sit there listening a long while, the imaginary waters washing him through.

MORNING

He settles on a hotel in the high-rise district. It is un-showy but adequate.

Apart from the nasty little sachets of coffee in his room everything is fine. Everything is orderly. Everything is neat and clean and compact. The drawers in the cabinet along the wall run smoothly on their tracks.

He can get back into a healthy routine. Sort his sleep pattern out. He reminds himself how long it has been since he's had a proper break and determines to make the most of the facilities the hotel has on offer. He has never, when staying at a hotel on business, made the most of the facilities.

His first morning he gets up with the alarm, showers, puts on his clothes, and slides open the two rice paper screens that stand in for curtains.

After claiming his breakfast in the lobby – he flashes the meal card that is part of his deal – he returns to the room and brushes his teeth assiduously. The time he has for cleanliness has increased, he tells himself. He licks his teeth after brushing to check for any hint of plaque.

He makes a thorough tour of the building, to establish exactly what is on-site. In the lobby he admires the chocolate stand and luxury shop and well-equipped pharmacy. One level up he acquaints himself with the variety of restaurants. He reads the menus, and considers what he might like to eat.

He visits the fitness centre on the fifth floor, and immediately determines to make good use of the hotel pool, which, when he surveys it, is empty. The only sign of life is a receptionist with whom he has to sign in and out, and from whom, he discovers, he must collect a bathing cap.

On the twenty-seventh floor he experiments with the view from his room. He has often stayed in high-rises but has rarely paused to take in the view, let alone examine its possibilities so thoroughly. Planting his chair up close to the window he could be sitting on the prow of a ship. He is so high up.

He pushes back and sits with legs outstretched, feet resting on the ledge that runs beneath the window. It is a clear day. Reflected in the multitude of blinking glass panes in the high-rise closest to him he can see the whole district: tower upon tower of steel and glass.

When he moves to the ledge and looks directly below he can see a tennis court not otherwise in view. It is some way down – perhaps an extension of the fitness centre on the fifth floor – but quite visible.

There is a lesson going on and he watches as a small boy struggles with an oversized racquet. Balls arrive in a hard, steady pulse and although he fails to hit them back they keep coming. The boy looks hopeless; his shoulders slump. The coach appears with a gizmo to suck up the balls. The whole thing starts over.

He has not thought of his own boy in a long while but he thinks about him now.

His bathroom is beige, and looks as though it hasn't been refurbished in some time. The shower head is old, the same sort he had in England as a kid, and made of the kind of plastic that always cracks when it is dropped. This one has been dropped.

The beige toilet, though not high-tech, is more than adequate.

The sink has the usual paraphernalia. Cotton balls and cotton buds and shower cap and nail files and razor and shaving gel. All the little bottles.

He examines the hair conditioner. He had not used it that morning and it is unlikely he will use it at all. He has always had a fine head of hair and prefers to travel with products of his own. For him there is a tipping point in any hotel that has to do with the quality of the coffee provided in your room and whether or not there is hair conditioner.

In his apartment he had, for a long while, stored a cache of products taken from the bathrooms of hotels in a clear plastic ziplock wash bag under his sink – for the use of anyone who might be staying over. As a rule they were very pleased. In this way he had discovered what he now considers a feature consistent in women – the cultish adoration of miniature bottles and tubes. He remembers returning to his bedroom to find a woman, naked, kneeling on the bed, reverently ordering them into rows.

In New York he had got used to using products from Kiehl's. He liked the old-fashioned feel of the shop – the fact that the business had been going so long. He enjoyed the shop assistants dressed as technicians or doctors in their white lab coats who would ask him endless questions about the requirements he personally had. He liked the specificity of what they offered and the lengthy descriptions on the labels of the bottles. He liked the fact they gave him sample bottles every visit that he made. He used them to refill the ziplock bag for his guests.

He swims in the empty pool in a pair of hotel Speedos. Floating on his back he looks up through a domed glass roof to the blue sky.

He falls into a deep sleep on a poolside lounger and on waking is confronted with a figure staring back at him from the mirrors up above, horizontal, inverted, startled, swathed in a white towelling gown with black bathing cap.

Is that me? he thinks.

In the mirror in the fitness centre washroom he watches himself sitting on a low plastic stool in a row of low plastic stools positioned in front of handheld showers and large dispensers of shampoo and conditioner and body wash. It is very quiet apart from the sound of bubbling coming from the hot tub. The stool he is on reminds him of a potty and he wonders how hygienic it is to plant your behind and genitals where others have done too; but the place stinks of chlorine in a way that suggests germs wouldn't survive.

In the washroom he has access not only to the hot bath but

also to a cold bath sitting alongside and to a sauna. A notice on the wall of the washroom informs him that he must clean himself before using any of it. Though it is clear that he must not wear bathing clothes there is no mention of whether he should keep on his snug black cap. As shampoo has been made available he assumes it is acceptable to take it off. In the mirror he can see a deep red groove running from one side of his forehead to the other where the elastic of the cap has dug in. It looks as though his skin has been scored over in preparation for some dramatic form of surgery.

He does not mind the stench of chlorine or the clinical atmosphere of the room. When he has peeled off his swimming trunks and hung them on the hook on the wall with his locker key and cap, when he has taken a seat on the low stool and propped his now fuggy glasses on the ledge in front of him, he feels absorbed in the task at hand.

He is already clean, he is sure, from his shower in the bathroom in his room and from the one he took at the entrance to the pool and no doubt from the swim itself which has left his eyes pricking with chlorine.

But he should clean himself before his hot bath; in this he agrees with the notice on the wall. He is more than happy to clean himself. The products have been made available. There is no one else in the room.

EVENING

They want to give him cocktails. He has a package that lets him claim pina coladas.

When he arrived and signed up, the man at the desk, with great diligence, filled in a cocktail card for every night of his stay, individually signed and dated, to be presented whenever he claimed his free drink. He can present only one card a night – they don't want him having all his drinks in one go.

He takes a corner table which affords him a good view of the lobby, and when they ask what he would like to drink he hands them his card.

First they set down a little white drinks mat, and then, on top of it, a pina colada with a chunk of pineapple attached to the rim, and finally a bowl of nuts. He sits there and drinks his pina colada and works his way through the little bowl of nuts. The cocktail is fairly weak but this does not bother him.

This is great, he tells himself; this is just what I need.

He is not bothered either by being alone. The central seating area where they serve food and drink has enough going on that a person would never feel self-conscious there simply for being alone: many people are. There are single men and women he can see who have come downstairs to eat or drink, some with a book, some with a laptop.

He decides to stay on in the lobby to eat. They have a good range of options on the menu.

And really, there is a lot happening. Clusters of people are gathered to meet – holidaymakers, film crews, minor rock stars even, he thinks, as well as all of those on more conventional business trips. He tries to figure it out from the clothes they have on. He tries to listen in on conversations though voices are rarely loud enough to hear, the tables positioned just far enough apart to be discreet.

He does not have a laptop or a mobile or a BlackBerry, or indeed a book. The book would have been an afterthought but the rest of the arsenal is standard for him. He notices that he doesn't know what to do with his hands, which is perhaps why the pina colada is welcome; though it is, he is aware, a ridiculous drink for a man. He could order something else but the cocktail is free, and he senses that he will enjoy the ritual of handing over the small piece of paper – something like a business card – that they have given him, that the man at the desk has so carefully filled in.

In his room he checks for messages and there are none. This is not surprising, although he still expects the phone to ring.

He puts the chair back up close to the window and looks out into darkness, tiny lights.

What do you do when you stop? When you have been up and running for such a long time, what is it you do? When you're used to a schedule that takes care of each second of the day? When there is no goal?

You scrub your skin. You sit on low stools and wash yourself.

MORNING

When he wakes up he feels that something is missing.

He opens his eyes to the room and then pictures the apartment in New York: the wide expanse of floor, the vast windows, and the view over the park.

His last night he had spent with a girl he'd seen once before. They had a parquet picnic in his living room. They got very drunk on a couple of bottles of fine wine.

Later the girl paraded around his room in nothing but his old-fashioned, old man's slippers. The curtains were drawn back from the windows. She recited, loudly, some thing about a bear hunt. Her arms swung back and forth like pendulums. She was laughing at him, he knew that, she was sending him up; but she looked so ridiculous he was laughing at her too.

The girl decided that since it was a sleepover they should move everything from the bed to the floor. They worked as a team on this. Their only disagreement was over the mattress which he argued for, she against.

'Alrighty, old man,' she had said.

In the night she had swatted him away with one lazy hand saying, 'That's enough from you.'

That's enough from you.

He had gone to the phone and booked himself on to a flight. He drank the last of the milk from the carton in the fridge. He got up early, left her sleeping in his sheets on the floor. He imagines her in the apartment, walking about when he is gone.

Now he shuffles to the bathroom in his white hotel slippers. 'Alrighty, old man,' he says to himself. 'That's enough.'

*

He has all these passes: the one he flashes for breakfast, the one that lets him in and out of his room, the one with a tick in the box for free gym membership that gives him access to the pool, and the one for cocktails.

There have always been passes. He pictures himself entering the building through the revolving doors and going into the main lobby, towards the barriers. He reaches the barriers. His pass is ready in his hand. He realises he has no idea where his pass comes from. Does he keep it in the back pocket of his pants along with his wallet, or inside his jacket, in an interior pocket? He doesn't know. The pass is just there in his hand. He holds it against the pass pad and he is through the barrier. But where does he put it then?

He arrives for his swim without the card with the box and the tick. The usually obliging young woman forbids him access; demands a not insignificant amount of cash upfront. She doesn't seem to recognise him. He goes back to his room, finds the box, and the tick, and returns to the desk. To his relief she lets him in.

In the pool he tries to concentrate on the movement of his arms, his legs, but this time he is not alone, and is distracted. There is another man. He is swimming a personalised back stroke which seems more like water-based t'ai chi. He times each stroke around a long, laboured out breath, and meanders to and fro, his shoulder-length white hair floating on the surface around him. When he's done, he shakes himself off at the side of the pool, grinning. Lurking in the shallow end Morris keeps his own mouth firmly shut. His eyes are transfixed by the body in decline: the sagging of the belly and breasts, the papery skin at the top of the thighs.

He thinks that maybe if he keeps his mouth shut for long enough his brain will re-programme. He thinks of the boy. He tries to recreate his face, like a jigsaw, because he cannot remember the whole.

EVENING

There is a bar attached to the lobby, though generally it lacks the sense of privacy and discretion so essential, in his mind, to a quiet, meaningful drink. In the mornings they use it to cater for the overflow of hotel guests who roll into the lobby to claim their all-you-can-eat buffet breakfast; who pile on to the leather armchairs, and overwhelm the tabletops with their heaped plates of pancakes and English Breakfasts and fruit bowls and pastries and litter the carpet with their crumpled napkins and crumbs; who talk loudly, and all at once; who shatter the eloquent calm of the wooden panelled walls and glowing cabinets of amber malts.

In the evening, the lobby thins out. He wanders into the bar and takes a seat.

Beside him a young man – and he strikes him as particularly young, perhaps barely shaving – is sitting and smoking with a look of worldliness that makes Morris want to ask what could possibly be weighing so heavily on his mind at his age. The young man is dressed for business, he has on a suit.

Morris has not bummed a smoke or sat with a drink and a cigarette at a bar since the ban kicked off in New York, but he gestures his request for a cigarette, and then accepts it with a nod. He doesn't recognise the brand. In the States he had always smoked Nat Sherman's. He liked the box they came in, all lined up.

A woman who had been a student of literature – a fellow smoker – once took him to a roadside motel for what she billed a 'dirty realist' weekend. In their room everything was dark brown except for the huge Jacuzzi in the bathroom, which was pink. The twin beds – it was the only room available, the place dubiously popular – were unpleasantly soft, with matching fringed, velveteen coverlets thrown over them. Everything smelled of cigarettes and air freshener.

He recalls a fresh-looking stain on the thick pile carpet. He recalls the big ashtray that was set on the small, ringed table in-between the beds. He recalls the continental breakfast of burnt coffee and doughnuts in slicked sugar.

Now he toys with the idea of requesting a smoker's room, imagines himself puffing away, looking out at the world from his chair. Instead he decides he will walk down the long corridor on one of the smoking floors, and breathe in the air.

Sitting at the bar he becomes aware of things he knows that two days ago he did not:

1. He knows that the silver button for the lift in the hotel will always give a static shock. Anticipation, he has discovered, makes it worse.
2. He knows that the kettle in his room is not at all straightforward and that in spite of time passing, he can't work it out. Each attempt he makes to use it is like the first time.

3. He knows now – somehow – that all through his working life he managed to avoid standing at the front of a
   crowded lift. He has no idea why, and he has no idea
   why he hasn't realised before.

4. He knows that in the pharmacy on the ground floor of
   the hotel they sell face masks. They have them hanging
   on a rack in front of the till. He will buy one, but not yet.

5. He knows now that without his BlackBerry, to check email
   he would have to pay 400 yen for fifteen minutes in the
   business centre on the ground floor. This is an absurdity.

6. He knows that he wants the phone to ring and expects
   it to ring and it doesn't ever ring.

There had been, he realises, an opportunity for paying attention to a person. There once had been an opportunity there for
care. The face he can't hold on to, the face that has unravelled,
a confused composite of a thousand other faces – this face that
he seeks; he has to give it up, because he chose to give it up a
long time ago and lost his right to it.

MORNING

Day three he goes up to the executive suites on the third floor:
takes in the air of quiet efficiency. Although it is early the offices
are filling up. Suits pass him along the corridor, disappear.

Through an open doorway he sees row upon row of men,
on their feet, lined up. He watches through the window,
through the thin slats of the blind. He sees them looking like
children, standing to attention, swinging their arms in unison,

jumping up and down in time, stretching to the left, to the right. He sees them follow – with great care – the instructions thrown at them; all together, in their suits, in the office, at the start of the day.

In the room opposite, which is unoccupied, he takes a seat behind the desk. He lets his palms fall on the arm rests, taking in the complimentary notepad, and pencils, and ballpoints, and the bottles of water, sparkling and still. He opens and closes the drawers to either side of him. Empty. He reaches out for the telephone. He picks up the receiver and listens to the hush at the other end, before putting it back down.

He folds his arms and sits back and closes his eyes. He remembers his own handsome, fitted desk, and the strange ergonomic chair in black, with its million-and-one levers and tilts and screws. He remembers the brassy, shining lift that took him up to the office, espresso in hand. He remembers the flowers in the lobby and the gleaming marble counter at the reception desk.

The boy had come to his office, alone, presented himself. It was more than a decade ago.

Morris had tried to locate him in women he remembered, but he remembered so little of the women that there wasn't a whole lot of point. Nevertheless he had been certain that the boy there in front of him, just across the desk from him, was his son.

He tried to assess his age. He had little experience of children but he guessed eleven, no more than twelve. The boy had not hit puberty. His skin had the glow of child about it, was clean and clear. His hair was cut short for summer. He sat upright and easy.

Morris had cast back as far as twelve years and tried to make a study of his long-lost catch, but there were only fragments, nothing coherent, nothing suggesting one moment over all the others, one person, one face.

A woman is standing in the doorway; tiny, immaculate. She is looking at him. Now she has his attention she nods briefly, bows. 'Can I help you, sir?' Her English is immaculate too. All in all she is as impeccable as Morris has learnt to expect all the staff at the hotel to be.

Caught off guard, he doesn't know how to respond. He pushes himself up from the desk and walks across the room to her, reaches out and clasps both of her hands in his. 'Thank you,' he says, looking her in the eye with great intent. And then he nods, bows, and leaves the room.

The door across the way has now been closed. Behind the blinds, the men are at their desks, heads bowed.

As he reaches the lift and steps inside, catching his reflection in the panels, he notices his clothes; the polo shirt and slacks, the navy jacket, the brogues. It was automatic. He had dressed for a business trip and packed for one.

The boy had sat there, in the office, just across the desk from him, full of certainty. Morris believed in cutting the crap. He was unsentimental about naming things as they are. He did everyone a favour. The boy left and did not come back.

In his room, on a piece of paper, he creates a grid, filling the boxes with activities available to him in the hotel: breakfast and swimming and the gym and the bar and the pharmacy and the chocolate stand and the luxury goods shop selling diamond-studded microphones and key rings. He has yet to visit the basement shopping complex. Last up he fills in smoking. And then he scores everything out and lies back on his bed.

Something bad is happening. There is a fizzing in his head and chest.

He wakes to find the T'ai Chi Swimmer breathing close to his face, trying to haul him from the sauna. He finds himself fixating on the chin which is hanging loose above him.

The T'ai Chi Swimmer sits panting on the rim of the cold bath outside. He takes up the scoop with the long handle and dips it into the water, pours it over his head. 'Man!' he says, and grins.

Morris looks down at his crumpled belly as he sits there on the plastic stool, studies the folds.

'I wonder what that was,' he says.

'Oh. You fainted,' the T'ai Chi Swimmer says. 'You fell down and hit your head.'

Morris rubs his eyes.

'How long had you been in there? You looked a little out of it when I arrived.'

'I don't know.' Morris shrugs. He has no recollection. He can't even remember going in.

'OK. Well – fifteen minutes max. But you have to build

to that,' the T'ai Chi Swimmer says. 'If I were you I'd drink some water. You need a hand?'

'No. No. Thanks.'

Morris heads through to the changing rooms. He has a drink from the cooler in the corner and takes a seat on one of the long benches in-between the lockers. He must have landed hard on one side of his face – his cheek is throbbing. He feels hot and nauseated.

EVENING

He sits in the lobby in his usual spot with a pina colada and small bowl of nuts.

The T'ai Chi Swimmer emerges out of nowhere. 'There you are!'

'Ah,' Morris says.

'Whoosh!' The T'ai Chi Swimmer drops himself on to the soft couch. He has given himself a centre parting since Morris saw him last: his evening look.

'Busy day?' Morris asks.

'Not as busy as you, old boy. Look at that.' His eyes have latched on to the bruise. 'Shiner!' As Morris takes a sip of his drink the T'ai Chi Swimmer looks at him with studied, surgical precision. 'How are you?'

'Fine.'

'No other adverse effects?'

'Not that I can tell.'

'Dizziness?'

'No.'

'Keep an eye. Care with concussion.'

Morris smiles weakly, tries to shift focus to attracting the attention of a waiter. Even with a cocktail card he must sign a receipt for his drink, and the sooner he can sign the sooner he can go.

But it is not a waiter who approaches their table. The woman is English. She is old. 'I wondered if I might join you two?' she says.

'Welcome! Welcome!' The T'ai Chi Swimmer throws up his hands. 'Join our little party!' She looks pleased, flushed, sinks on to the sofa beside him. She has added a streak of mauve, Morris notices, to her hair. 'I'm Jane.'

'Pleasure! Anthony.' They shake hands. 'And this is—'

'Jeremy,' Morris says. He takes a deep breath. He tries to sound gracious. 'What can I get you both?'

'I'll have what you're having,' Anthony says.

'Pina colada,' he hears himself explaining. 'It comes with my package.'

'Your package?' Anthony smiles from ear to ear. 'Oh-kay. I'll pass on that. Get me a Corona. Wedge of lime.'

'I'll have an Ice Cream Song,' Jane says, pointing at the specials.

'That's right!' Anthony cries. 'Throw caution!'

Morris sits there with his pina colada. They both suck at their drinks.

'Best medicine, right?' A wink from Anthony. 'So, Jeremy, what's your line of work?'

It takes him a moment to realise the question is for him. 'Oh, this and that,' he says.

Anthony swigs from his bottle, changes tack. 'OK, so tell me about your *package*,' he says. '*What* is the deal there?'

They ask him about his accent. They wonder whether he is English or American. He tells them he gets that a lot.

'Like Cary Grant,' Jane says, and blushes.

'Steady on!' Anthony laughs.

Jane has noticed crossover in English and American. Computers spell in American, she finds. It is frustrating – she no longer knows which spelling is which, which way round things go, doesn't know if she's writing in English. She used to be an English Language teacher, which makes it very embarrassing! Jane laughs quietly – a breath through her nose.

Anthony sells models of vintage cars. Since retirement he has expanded online. 'Must be fascinating,' Morris says. Anthony has left the shop in his daughter's hands. She was always into automobiles. 'Unusual,' Jane says. 'For a girl.'

He imagines his son visiting the apartment. The girl is still there.

He is older now – grown up – but his hair is the way it was then; a fine, fair stubble over his scalp, a summer crop, the shape of his head neat and smooth beneath. His eyes are a translucent blue.

The girl makes him coffee at the breakfast bar, watching him walk around. He goes out to the balcony and she finds him there, resting his elbows on the ledge. He takes the coffee, smiles at her. Together they look out over the park.

They are talking, but Morris cannot hear what they are saying.

'Okay, now, driving in America, right?!' This addressed to him.

'Aha?' He stirs in his seat, uncertain of what has been implied.

'Although they all drive automatics, right? Where's the pleasure in that?'

Morris had never learnt to drive. He could never see the point. People would always say, 'You're in America, you *can't not* drive.' As though driving on endless interstates was something unmissable.

'I never learnt to drive,' he says. He enjoys telling people this. Anthony looks shocked. Men always look shocked – as though a vital part of his anatomy must be missing. He was too young to learn when there was anyone around who might have taken the time. And then it was New York. 'In Manhattan,' he says, 'you don't need a car. You walk or you take a cab.' He wonders when to leave. He tries to visualise the room service menu. He wants something in a bun: carbs.

'I always fancied the subway,' Jane says. 'It sounds so much better than the Tube!'

'Maaan-haaaten.' Anthony blinks and beams and stretches his arms all at once.

*

As Morris brushes his teeth, he looks into the mirror in the bathroom, the harsh light startling his skin. There was something cavalier about his face that he had always liked and it has disappeared. He is not sure what will replace it. He does not feel in control at all. He notices a new puffiness.

He remembers a lover telling him that Catherine Deneuve had put on weight to make herself look young. He can't remember the face of his lover any more but he can remember her showing him a magazine, holding it up, putting it right in front of him. 'Look. Look. Look at her face,' she had said, with a sense of urgency. 'Don't you see?'

His face is morphing – absorbing, perhaps, the chlorine of the swimming pool, the various unknown unguents that sit in the changing room for general use, and all the little bowls of nuts and pina coladas too. He examines his midriff – but does not think he is putting on weight overall. He does not think so.

'Hey buddy,' he says to himself in the mirror.

He had his idea of the way things should be. He had believed in letting a person go. He had believed it to be an act of some grace. Was that true? Was that even true? He had believed it was the way to hold on to the best part of them, believed in that moment of impact, right at the start – when their strangeness hit you, when you saw them clearly, when you took in all at once their shape, the way they stood, their hands, their skin, their eyes, when the air was full of them, when the world stopped for them, when if there were words the words would be, Hold it, hold it right there.

Or maybe the words would be, Don't come any closer.

He's back in the apartment. His son is a boy again, waiting for him, sitting and drinking from a carton of milk. He has with him a backpack and nothing in it but a spare pair of clothes and a toothbrush for staying over.

'Hey buddy,' he says.

His son is gabbling, telling him news of what he's been up to, the things he has done.

Acknowledgements

I gratefully acknowledge the financial support of both the Arts and Humanities Research Council and the University of Chichester in the development of this collection.

For their enthusiasm and expertise as I explored the short story form and worked towards a collection: Alison MacLeod, Stephanie Norgate and Andrew Cowan, and all the editors who have shown support for my work, especially Ra Page, Brendan Barrington, Nicholas Royle, Jacques Testard and Philip Langeskov.

Cathryn Summerhayes at WME.

Laura Macaulay, Karen Maine and Natasha Davis at Daunt Books.

Helen Simpson.

L. J. Mays, who introduced me to the short story.

Mahesh Rao.

My friends, fellow writers, and readers, for wisdom, perspective, humour and inspiration: you know who you are, and I am lucky, for you are many.

My family: with love and gratitude.

M. Roseveare: for everything. This book is for you.

The following stories have been previously published, although a number have since been revised: 'The Lake Shore Limited' in the *Dublin Review*, 'The Shallows' in *Lighthouse*, 'Rehearsal Room' in the *White Review*, 'By the Canal' in the *Sunday Times Magazine*, 'The Inland Sea' by Daunt Books. Some of the stories have been published in anthologies: 'The Lake Shore Limited' in *Best British Short Stories 2015*, edited by Nicholas Royle (Salt), 'Blackout' in *What Lies Beneath: A Collection of Short Stories from the Kingston Writing School*, selected by Bonnie Greer and Hilary Mantel (Kingston University Press), 'The Ice Cream Song is Strange' in *Edgeways*, the London Short Story Prize 2013 anthology, edited by Courttia Newland (Flight Press), 'The Human Circadian Pacemaker' in the BBC National Short Story Award 2011 anthology (Comma Press) and in the Bridport Prize 2010 anthology (Redcliffe Press Ltd), 'By the Canal' (excerpt) in *Cheque Enclosed*, the UEA Creative Writing Anthology 2007 (UEA). 'The Human Circadian Pacemaker' was broadcast on BBC Radio Four in September 2011.

Arts & Humanities
Research Council